The Mistletoe Feud

The Mistletoe Feud

A ROMANTIC COMEDY NOVEL

DANIELLE MORRIS

ISBN 979-8-9876836-2-0

Developmental Editing/Proofreading by Haley Warren & Esther Godoy Montanez

Cover image by Erika Plum IG @custombyerikaplum

Author Photo by Zachary Morris

Chapter headings/scene break graphics by Canva

Follow me on Instagram @daniellemorriswrites for more updates on future books!

For my favorite team of weasels:

Esther & Haley

Thanks for cheering me on and believing in my writing every step of the way.

And to the weasel husbands,

Spur-Fingers, Brown Bear, and Bennifer Squash

For listening to our unhinged voicenotes on an everyday basis and still loving us.

AUTHOR'S NOTE

Dear reader,

Thank you so much for picking up my book. I truly hope you find something that resonates with you when you read it. That being said, I know this book deals with some very heavy topics that might be triggering for some of you. There's only one of you in this world, and I firmly believe in taking care of yourself first—forever and always.

I've listed some content warnings below for those who might need them.

- Open door spice

- Explicit language

- Mentions of infidelity (misunderstanding)

I hope you find some of yourself scattered throughout this story. My whole heart is on these pages, and it means the world to me that you've picked this book up and are giving it a chance.

Love always,

Danielle

CHAPTER ONE

Phoebe

"**P**heebs, you have to be there. You're literally not allowed to leave me hanging when I'm flying from freaking Germany to be there for Christmas! I'll pull the twinster card on your ass so fast," Piper threatens loudly, making me want to shrink and hide anywhere but the quiet library I'm currently huddled up in.

"Piper, shut up! I told you I was in the library!" I whisper-yell at my sister and risk a glance over at Mrs. Jones, the cranky librarian, and I cringe when I see the daggers she's throwing my way with those unfriendly icy blue eyes. Mrs. Jones has thrown me out of this library several times, and I know she's 'jonesing' to do it again. I swallow an ugly snort because Dad would be proud of that stupid dad joke.

I miss my parents so much. I haven't seen them in the last year, and the last time I saw them was less-than-pleasant. Not to mention, it really solidified my angsty feelings about the holidays.

Christmas was always my favorite time of the year. I grew up in a small town called Noelsville, nestled near the foot of the Appalachian Mountains in North Carolina. Noelsville always went all out for the holidays. Carts in the town square sold delicious sweets and hot cocoa. They have a Christmas parade and an epic Christmas Market that the town locals put together every year.

I've always looked forward to all the twinkling lights and the snow-dusted porches. There was magic in the air to go along with all the perfectly shaped evergreen trees shining brightly through all the large bay windows. Everyone spends their days baking cookies and picking out the perfect holiday cards to send to all their family and friends. The holiday feasts Mom would create each year, decorating cookies with my twin sister, sneaking pieces of candy off of the gingerbread house with my little brother, Dad kicking our asses at cards.

Those are some of my favorite memories. Christmas was my freaking jam.

That is, until my boyfriend of four years decided to dump me on Christmas Eve last year. At his house...*in front of my entire family*.

I hadn't gone home for Christmas in years, much to my dismay, but also out of sheer loyalty to my sister. Piper is in the military, and getting her leave approved around the holidays has always been difficult. It didn't feel right to celebrate at home without her. When I met Kevin, he didn't see the point in traveling for the holidays. He hated the crowded airports and traffic and always complained that he traveled enough for work and didn't want to spend his time off stressing about traveling even more. So, instead of going home, Kevin and I invited my family to celebrate with us at his place in New York.

It was the first time my family had traveled to us for the holidays, and I was so excited to show off all the decorating I had done in Kevin's house. I went all out. We had cinnamon-scented pinecones set up, and it smelled like Christmas the minute you walked in the front door. The tree was 7 feet tall and decorated to perfection. Each bulb was carefully placed, and the lights were perfectly spaced between the golden tinsel garlands. The fireplace had stockings hung and filled with goodies for each of us. Yes, I might have filled my own because Kevin had forgotten. But that was okay, because my family was coming, and spending Christmas with them was more important than waiting for him to fill my stocking with mini bags of Hot Cheetos and fun holiday socks.

Kevin decided he no longer wanted to be with me somewhere between cutting the Christmas ham and getting ready to exchange gifts. My parents and brother, Phillip, three years younger than Piper and I, were all getting settled around the tree when Kevin asked if he could speak to me outside. I remember the twinkle in Mom's eyes when I excused myself and followed him. I think she expected the same thing I was—an engagement ring.

Instead, he dumped me with the typical 'it's not you, it's me' excuse, and then, to add salt to the wound, he asked if I could leave and take my family back to my tiny apartment in Queens.

Cue the sad girl music and too many bowls of Rocky Road. And a new hatred for the holiday. Just call me Miss Scrooge. He not only ripped my heart to shreds, but he took away my love for Christmas.

I honestly don't know which one is worse.

As I said, my family has always gone all out for the holidays, which is probably where my intense love for this season came from. When we were kids, my parents and our neighbors, Mr. and Mrs. Larson, would put together these wild contests for all the kids, like actual contests. The winners were even crowned at the end of the five-day competition. My sister Piper always won, and I'm still pretty salty that I never got to wear the coveted Mistletoe Crown. It was like a full-blown prom-like king and queen coronation in the neighbor's backyard, except there was only one winner. I may not have ever won the whole thing, but my ugly sweaters were epic, and I never lost that one.

Five of us always competed: myself, my sister Piper, our brother Phillip, and the neighbors' two sons, Spencer and Austin.

Spencer is a year older than Pipes and I, and he was obnoxiously gorgeous in high school and the first guy I ever really fell for. I had a crush on him for my entire childhood, but we all know that those kinds of love stories never last. It doesn't help that I ghosted him after watching him kiss my sister at our Winter Formal. While being *my* date. Piper pulled me into the bathroom afterward and told me he kissed her out of nowhere and that she couldn't pull away fast enough.

I never confronted him about it; I just left the dance and completely stopped talking to him because I was so embarrassed and humiliated that he would kiss my sister after asking me to be his date. It's not like I wouldn't have let him kiss me; I was head over heels in love with the kid for crying out loud. He tried to talk to me a few times after that, but I made sure to steer clear of him at all costs. I didn't want an apology. I wanted a time machine.

After that, though, we purposely avoided each other for the rest of the school year. When Spencer graduated and left for college, I never had a reason to see him again. I guess I have this innate skill for falling for douchebags.

Austin is Phil's age, and they've been best friends for as long as I can remember. We always called them the terrorsome twosome when they were together. They both had a knack for pranking us when we were younger. I'm sure they still have that stupid video camera with all the recorded pranks they pulled on us. I know one is roaming around with me screeching like an eagle because they filled a balloon with whipped cream and marbles—and set it up to fall perfectly on my head as I came home from swim practice one evening. Why marbles, you ask? So it would fall hard enough to pop open all over my head and face—the little weasels.

"Earth to Phoebe? Are you still there or busy doing that disassociating thing you do?" I look down at my phone, and the only thing I can see is my sister's earlobe, which is looking back at me.

"You know we are on Facetime, right? You don't have to put the phone to your ear."

"I know! I was trying to hear if Mrs. Jones was yelling at you yet," Piper says smugly. "Anyway, I won't get you kicked out today. I'm just reminding you that you can't skip out on Christmas. I'm fully prepared to leak that video of you singing horribly to Taylor Swift in the shower if you don't show up."

"Dude, I was like ten. I don't care if you leak it." I roll my eyes at her and duck into an empty aisle near the back of the library. The further away I stay from Mrs. Jones, the better.

"Oh, you'll care about this, my stone-hearted little Medusa. Phil recorded it after Kevin dumped you last year. I'm pretty sure you don't want anyone to hear your horrible rendition of 'You Belong With Me.'"

I feel all the color drain from my face in horror because I remember precisely what moment she's talking about. I swear I'm going to murder our little brother when I see him.

"Fine. I'll see you next week, only because I miss Mom and Dad. The rest of you suck," I whisper angrily. "And honestly, of all the stupid nicknames you've come up with for me over the years, I think I like this 'Medusa' one the best. Also, you better delete that video, or you're getting buried next to Phillip!" I threaten her in my most serious voice, and instead of responding, she laughs loudly over the speaker before hanging up on me.

"Ms. Andrews..." I wince as I hear Mrs. Jones' voice getting closer to me. I leave quickly before Mrs. Jones finds me and throws me out again.

I step out into the blistering cold that has completely taken over the city and head towards the subway to head home for the night. I mentally start tallying everything I need to get in order before I fly out next week. I suppose I should look at flights, and I need to call my parents and tell them that I'm coming home for Christmas this year. The art museum I work at is pretty relaxed about us taking leave, even at the last minute, so that's one less thing I'll have to worry about. I need to wrap the gifts I've bought for everyone and buy a big enough suitcase to pack them all in.

Most importantly, though, I need to stop at the craft store because I have the best idea for this year's ugly Christmas sweater.

CHAPTER TWO

Spencer

I feel like I'm the Grinch standing in the town of Whoville. Santa's little elves are all around me, dressed in red and green outfits with candy cane-striped socks, pointed ears, and jingling shoes. Everyone is running around with checklists and happy-go-lucky smiles on their faces.

I can't believe I let my parents rope me into setting up this year's Christmas market. I should have known the moment the school went on Winter Break that my mom would guilt trip me into spending my vacation volunteering. She looks at me with those big brown puppy dog eyes, and I'm putty in her hands. Yes, that must sound creepy since she's my mom, but making her happy makes me happy. So, I'm just being selfish.

"Hey, Spencer!" I hear my name shouted from somewhere, but I can't place whose voice it is. Setting the box of lights on the ground in front of me, I lift my hand to my eyes to block the sun's bright rays and look around the fairgrounds.

"Spence, over here!" I turn quickly toward the voice, and my heart stops when I finally see her. Phoebe. The biggest and only 'what if' of my life. The girl I royally screwed things up with when I was a senior in high school when her twin sister and I got caught kissing.

"What's up Spen-Sirrrrr!" Her voice comes out in a mock-ing-sing, songy tone.

And just like that, I realize that I've messed up again. *That stupid nickname.* Only one person has called me that, and it's not Phoebe. I have to force myself from physically recoiling when Piper finally reaches me and throws her arms around me. I haven't spoken to her much since that night at the Winter Formal—the night we ruined any chance I had with Phoebe. Even if I had wanted to reach out and explain to Phoebe what had happened, I couldn't have.

And she hasn't come home since she left for college in New York...five years ago.

Piper squeezes herself closer to my body, and small knots of dread form in my stomach.

What if Phoebe is here? What if she sees Piper embracing me like I'm her long-lost lover?

I pull back quickly and nervously shove my hands into the pock-ets of my jeans. "Hey, Piper. How's military life treating you? Are you home for the holidays?" I ask her, though I don't care to hear her answer. I can't help the tiny sliver of hope blooming in my stomach as I look around for Phoebe.

"She's not coming until tomorrow," Piper says instead of answering my questions.

My eyes widen as I look back at her. I can feel the start of a blush creeping up my neck. Am I that obvious?

"Yes, you are," Piper teases as a knowing smirk tugs at her lips as she answers my unspoken thoughts. She puts her hands on her hips and looks me up and down like she's sizing me up. I feel about two feet tall when her eyes reach mine again.

How could I ever confuse these two?

Phoebe and Piper may be identical twins, but they are also completely and totally different. Piper's green eyes are a couple of shades brighter than her twins, and they have always looked a bit hostile like she's ready to rip you a new one the moment you look her way. Phoebe's eyes look like someone plucked dark emeralds from a treasure chest, and a thin, golden ring surrounds her irises. Both sisters have always been short, but Piper was slightly shorter than Phoebe the last time I saw them together, and both had the same slim and petite bodies. Except now Piper looks more solid and more muscular. Her face has taken on some sharper angles and lost that teenager look. She's also packed on some serious gains, which, being in the military, a bit of muscle makes sense for her.

"Are you done ogling me? Or should I tell Pheebs you're still a douchebag?"

"Jesus, Piper," I pinch the bridge of my nose. "I'm not a douchebag. I'm not checking *you* out, and you *know* it." My voice is low as I emphasize my words and give her a hard stare. I can't help but get a small thrill of pleasure when I see her eyes widen a fraction in surprise. Her entire demeanor changes with my words, and I watch as she swallows hard and runs a nervous hand through her hair. It's cropped short to her shoulders, and her natural shade of red has been dyed dark brown.

I guess she thought if she avoided me long enough, I'd forget about our past—no such luck when she and her sister were both back home for the first time in years.

"You couldn't wait ten minutes before you threw that in my face. Really, Spence?" Her bright green eyes are lined with annoyance, but she's tugging at the sleeves of her black jacket, so I know she's nervous about me spilling the beans.

Which I wouldn't do.

I still care about Phoebe too much to hurt her even further than we already have. The look on her face when she saw Piper and me kissing still haunts me. I'll do everything in my power to make sure I never have to see that look of devastation and betrayal in her eyes again.

Except tell her the truth.

I clear my throat in an obvious way to ease the tension I just created between us. I don't hate Piper. I never have. She was one of my closest friends when we were kids. She was the only one who didn't laugh at me when I had to get braces in middle school, and she went with me to all the school dances because I was too nervous to ask Phoebe to go with me. Piper never wanted to go to the dances, as she was not about that social life at all and would have lived happily ever after with an anime comic and her punk-rock music blasting too loudly from her headphones. But, she sucked it up and always said yes because she knew that her going would be the only way to get Phoebe to go too.

I could say that Piper was my wingwoman. Unfortunately, she also helped me ruin any shot I had with her sister back then.

In one stupid move, I lost the girl of my dreams and my best friend.

And even though it'll be hard to see Phoebe tomorrow, I've really missed having Piper in my life.

I should probably work on separating the children we were from the adults we are now.

Piper must be doing her mind-reading thing again because one moment, we're awkwardly staring at each other in the middle of Whoville, and the next, she's punching me in the arm. Hard, I might add. "I missed you too, Spen-Sirrrr."

"I hate that nickname," I gripe. Piper's smile is infectious, and I feel the corners of my lips curl up.

"I know, but I love saying it." She looks down at the box of Christmas lights and then around the mostly set up market. By tonight, the market should be ready for business. "Let's hang these lights so we can go get lunch. I can't wait to hear all about this teaching thing you've got going on now, Mr. Larson. That sounds so freaking professional." She beams proudly up at me before she continues. "And I know you're dying to hear all about my gorgeous and single sister." She tries to throw a wink my way, but I can't contain the loud laughter that erupts from my chest at the sight of it. Piper's winks are just a rapid succession of blinks.

"Five years later, you still can't do a proper wink!" I tease her, and she rolls her eyes at me while flipping the bird. I swat at her hand like a child and reach down to grab the box of lights before that last bit she said clicks in my brain. "Wait, did you say Phoebe is single? What happened to that banker dude she was dating?"

"First off, it's creepy that you've been cyber-stalking my sister. Secondly, just because he lives in New York doesn't automatically make him a banker," she replies.

"What did he do then?"

"I have no idea. I didn't like him enough to ask. But who cares about that douchebag. Now let's go, Romeo. I'll tell you all about what's new with Pheebs *after* you buy me a beer."

I know I shouldn't let myself get excited. Nothing has changed between us, and I've let five years of resentment build on Phoebe's shoulders. She hates me, and I can't tell her what happened without risking ruining her relationship with her sister.

But I'd be lying if I said I wasn't excited to see her again.

CHAPTER THREE

Phoebe

The plane has finally gotten under the thick layer of fluffy white clouds, and the sky is a perfect shade of baby blue. I have my face pressed close against the cold window as I desperately try to spot my parents' house from above—a useless task since every house looks identical. All I can make out are rows and rows of perfect little boxes, each surrounded by white snow, and most of the chimneys have little puffs of smoke coming out of them.

I can't believe I've spent so long away from this place. My knee bounces wildly in anticipation as the plane approaches the ground. I'm ready to breathe in the smells of my home and hug my parents tightly. I'm even excited to see my siblings, though they're still on my naughty list.

Only Piper could guilt trip me into returning, and only Phil could have the means to help her.

I can't believe that little weasel recorded me singing my heartache out with Taylor Swift. I've got to find a way to get him to erase that stupid video. I don't need any reminders of how badly Kevin broke my heart a year ago.

The flight attendant announces over the intercom that we're preparing to land, and I'm more than ready to comply with her list of demands so we can get out of this sardine can and back on steady ground. Flying doesn't typically bother me, but I've felt extra anxious about this trip home since Piper told me Spencer was volunteering at the town Christmas Market. Of course, she would run into him the minute she landed. You'd think she'd have better things to do, like, I don't know, sleep so that she could adjust to the vast time difference between here and Germany.

When she texted me and told me they were going out for lunch, my stomach twisted and turned into a green-eyed monster of a mess. It's been five years. Why am I still so jealous of her hanging out with him?

I walked out on him.

I chose not to let him explain his side of the story because I couldn't handle the fact that he liked my sister more than he liked me. They were inseparable all throughout our lives, and I always had this feeling that he wanted her. It makes no sense why he asked me to be his date unless I was just an easier version of her that seemed attainable since Piper had always made it clear she only thought of him as a friend.

Earth to Phoebe, you're still worried about that because deep down, you'll never really let go of that childhood crush you've had on Spencer your whole life.

I'm so lost in my thoughts that I don't realize how close we are to the ground when the plane lands roughly. A startled scream escapes my throat, and I grab onto the armrests of my seat as the plane hops on the runway several times. It sways back and forth until the pilot can slow the plane to a steady glide. Everyone starts clapping as we pull up to our gate. I never really understood why clapping at the end of the plane ride was a thing, but I join my fellow passengers because I'm so ready to get out of this plane.

A half-hour later, I finally see my zebra-printed suitcase getting dropped onto the luggage carousel. I send a quick text to Piper to let her know to come pick me up outside of the baggage claim doors. I really should've just taken a carry-on, but I didn't want to mess up the supplies for the epic ugly Christmas sweater I had wrapped carefully in my bag. Not to mention, the Christmas gifts I have for the family definitely wouldn't have fit in a carry-on.

Waiting on luggage after a flight is reminiscent of being on the diving pad at a swim meet, waiting on the high-pitched tone of the whistle to signal the start of the race. Everyone around me waits to charge when the carousel lets out a loud beep, indicating it's being turned on. I patiently wait my turn, watching as my bag gets closer, but as I step forward to grab it, someone else beats me to it. I have to reign in a gasp when this tall stranger turns around with my suitcase in his hands.

Spencer freaking Larson.

My mind goes completely blank as I stare up at him. I'm too focused on his lips and how they move as he speaks to me. He still looks like the same Spencer I knew five years ago, but my goodness, he has aged like a fine wine. He's still tall, but his arms and shoulders are broader and *much* more muscular. The red and green flannel he's wearing fits tightly across his chest, and I vaguely wonder if he still hits the gym regularly. My eyes wander up and down his body, and I feel the moisture in my mouth completely dry up as I chew on my bottom lip.

This is so unfair. Spencer is still absolutely gorgeous, and looking up at his bright hazel eyes, I genuinely wish I could shut off the nagging voice that's telling me to stay away from him.

Stay far, far away, Phoebe.

"PHEEBS!"

Hearing that voice, I feel like a bucket of ice water has been tossed on me. I turn towards the annoyingly loud screech that belongs solely to my sister as she tackles me from behind and throws me right into a Spencer-Piper hug sandwich.

It's easy to tell that pesky voice in the back of my head to screw off when I'm pressed this close to Spencer's muscular body, with his broad arms wrapped tightly around my body. It's almost like he's protecting me from the onslaught of my sister, and I can't say I'm upset about it. My face is pressed flush with his chest, and I can't stop myself from inhaling the scent of him. A girls gotta breathe, right? He smells like cinnamon, with notes of evergreen. He smells like a Christmas tree, A delicious six-foot-tall Christmas tree.

You know that saying, 'I'd climb that man like a tree?' Well, it's never really made sense to me until right now, Right at this moment, while being forced to snuggle up to the guy I've crushed on for my whole life—that saying finally makes total sense.

Spencer clears his throat loudly between us, and I feel the vibration of it flow through my entire body. I feel Piper laughing against my back, and I'm suddenly reminded that we're not alone. We're in the middle of the airport. I cannot let myself get all hot and bothered, especially while being sandwiched between the guy I'm supposed to hate for breaking my teenage heart and my sister for helping that happen.

Nope.

I don't like this.

I don't like this *at all*.

I actually hate everything about this, and I want to wring my sister's perfect neck for bringing him here. I don't blame her for anything that happened between them, but seeing them together isn't easy for me. I wish I could just go back in time and completely scrub the memory of their kiss out of my brain.

I push myself, maybe a little too roughly, away from Spencer's chest and turn around to give my traitorous sister an actual hug. "I really hate you right now, but I missed your stupid matching face so much," I whisper to her and hug her tighter against me. I can't believe I haven't seen her since she moved to Germany three years ago. "And because I'm more happy to see you than upset to see him, I'm going to take the high road and forgive you for letting that whole 'Phoebe sandwich' happen."

She pulls back to wipe at her eyes, and I realize I'm on the verge of crying right along with her. She may rattle my chain like no one else can, but my heart is never whole when we're apart.

"I missed you too, and I have half a mind to drag you back overseas with me," Piper says with a tearful smile.

"Don't tempt me, Pipes. I may tuck and roll into your suitcase when it's time to leave." I genuinely hate this phase of our lives.

Of course, I'm so unbelievably proud of her, but I wish she had chosen to become a nurse without having to join the Air Force and being forced to live so far away from me. I've never been the strong one, and Piper has always been my rock. This last year has been so rough without her to lean on.

"Umm, ladies. Are you ready to head to the car yet?" Spencer asks while he steps around from behind me, with my suitcase still in his hand.

Piper and I glance up at him and then look at each other with wide, guilty eyes. A smile pulls at my lips, and I can see her matching smile. I cover my mouth with my hand quickly, and then we start laughing hysterically—because we both forgot that Spencer was still here with us.

CHAPTER FOUR

Spencer

Well, there isn't anything awkward about this situation at all. I'm just a six-foot-two guy sitting in the back of a small car with two identical-looking women singing loudly along with the radio in the front seat. Typically, this might seem like the start of an excellent joke or a very naughty dream, but when the two women in question haven't said a word to you since they left the airport, well, simply put–it's incredibly awkward.

I didn't expect Phoebe to speak to me at all. But when Piper asked me to tag along with her to the airport, I hoped it meant that she had talked to her sister and that maybe, just maybe, Phoebe would call a stalemate on her hatred for me.

For about forty-five seconds after I surprised Phoebe in the baggage claim, it looked like she might actually deign to speak to me again. That spark I've always felt for her was still there, and when I saw her standing there waiting for her bag, I couldn't stop myself from gravitating towards her.

It was like one of those golden strands from the Fates was pulling me towards her.

Then, we made eye contact for the first time in five years, and she took my breath away. She's even more beautiful than I remembered. Her eyes are nothing like the emeralds I recall them looking like. They are infinitely more stunning than the finest cut gemstones in the universe. They look like somebody bottled up the Aurora Borealis in Alaska and let them shine brightly out of her eyes. The rosy flush of her cheeks and the way she bit her lip while looking at me—I thought the possibility of starting fresh with her was in my grasp. That is until Piper decided to tackle her sister right in my chest before I could even say hello.

I knew the moment Phoebe stepped out of my arms, the spark in her eyes would be gone again. She's made eye contact with me several times since, and each glance looks guarded and unsure. And she has every right to look at me like that, even if it crushes me.

So now, I'm scrunched up in the back of Piper's rental car, and the street to our parents' house can't get here fast enough. At least the view is nice, and I don't mean that in some weird, creepy dude way, like I'm talking about the women in the front seat. I'm not.

The town has every light pole strung up with colorful Christmas lights, each with a ginormous wreath attached near the top. The sidewalks are lined with those plastic candy canes that light up from within, which adds to that Whoville effect the town seems to be going for every year. The snow falls lightly from the sky, making everything look magical and Christmasy. The sun has just started to set, so the sky is cast in dark blue, pink, and orange hues. The snow coming down makes the giant decorated tree in the middle of the town square look like something plucked right out of a snow globe.

"Hey Spencer, do you want anything from Lucene's? My mom just texted and asked if we could pick up some pizza and pasta for dinner," Phoebe asks me from the front. I'm momentarily shocked as I'm pulled out of my thoughts, and I'm positive if she turned to look at me right now, all she'd see is my mouth gaping open and closed like a fish.

"Earth to Romeo, my sister asked if you want pizza," Piper pipes in, and I catch her not-so-subtle wink aimed at me in the rearview mirror.

I glare back at Piper just in time for Phoebe to turn around and finally look at me. Her eyes widen quickly in surprise before her features settle back into that 'can't be bothered to care' face she tends to have around me.

"No, he doesn't want anything. Let's drop him off first and then go pick the food up. I want to say hi to Mom and Dad anyway," Phoebe answers annoyedly. Crap, she must think that my angry face was directed at her. I open my mouth to apologize to her, but no words form. She cocks an eyebrow at me and then faces back towards her sister.

What is it about her that makes me go full-on stupid anytime I'm within five feet of her? At this rate, I might as well give up and go home. It's not exactly fun being around someone who obviously still hates your guts.

"Actually," Phoebe says after looking at her phone, "The Larsons are coming over for dinner. Austin texted me to tell you to order 'the usual' for them."

"I guess it's a good thing I'm still here then," I mutter at her under my breath, feeling annoyed for continuing to torture myself by trying to get on her good side.

Phoebe turns around and cocks her eyebrow up again, right along with that annoyed look she gets in her eyes when she's done with someone. I think she thinks doing that makes her look intimidating or something, but it just makes me want to smile.

If I pretend hard enough, it feels like we are kids again, arguing over the best pizza toppings. I've forgotten how much I used to love riling her up when she would get that look in her eyes.

So that's exactly what I do. I flash her the biggest smile as I cross my arms over my chest. That makes her adorably-cocked eyebrow turn into a full-on death stare. Which is precisely the type of reaction I was hoping to coax out of her. From now on, I'm giving up this whole 'walking on eggshells' thing. If she wants to dish it out, she'll get it right back in the nicest way possible.

Now that I've settled on not trying to grovel for a scrap of her attention, I feel much happier being here. I may not get back on her good side, but I'll have fun getting under her skin while she's home.

She hasn't broken eye contact with me yet, which has to count for something, right? Piper is utterly clueless about the showdown happening in this car as she sings loudly along to *Three Days Grace*. The tension between Phoebe and me is at a nuclear level, and it takes every ounce of self-discipline not to reach down and adjust my pants. She's hot as hell when she's angry. And by the way, her fist is clenched on her lap, and the tick of her jaw is grinding back and forth. She's *definitely* angry at me.

We stay locked in this 'battle to the death' stare-down until Piper pulls into Lucene's parking lot. She glances over at her sister and then back at me before she gets out of the car and slams the door loudly on us. Leaving us alone in this compact car with "I Hate Everything About You" screaming from the speakers. It's oddly fitting for this moment.

Phoebe doesn't break her stare, meaning there's no chance I am either. Her lips part slightly, and I find myself bracing for the words getting ready to come out of her mouth. It'll be the first time she's spoken to me in five years because I don't count her asking if I want food as our first conversation. That was just politeness. The words she speaks now will be because she *wants* to speak them.

She unclenches her fist and shakes her hand out quickly. Then she finally breaks eye contact with me and grabs her purse. "Come on. Pipes can't carry all the food herself," she says, exiting the car.

That didn't go as planned.

CHAPTER FIVE

Phoebe

I *must not fall for Spencer Larson.*

I will not fall for Spencer Larson.

Please, for the love of Christmas, do not make it easy to fall for Spencer *freaking* Larson. I repeat this mantra the whole drive home while pretending not to be tied up in knots over how he smiled at me. It's unfair for him to be this good-looking and have that total panty-dropping smile.

The smile that turns my brain into a useless pile of putty. I almost told him I missed him and was glad he was here. I came to my senses at the last minute, though, and my sassy side came back out. It seems to be my default setting around him now. I'm either ready to fall into his arms and let him have his way with me, or I'm ready to punch him in that stupid, handsome face of his.

When we were younger, seeing Spencer walk up the front steps to our house made my heart flutter. I couldn't wait to squeeze between him and Piper on the couch as we watched the *Aliens* movies repeatedly. But after the Winter Formal and watching them lock lips—being stuck in this tiny car with them makes me want to scream.

Run far away while screaming.

I haven't paid attention to anything that Piper and Spencer have said during this short drive back to my parent's house, and I'm surprised when I feel a light tap on my shoulder. I turn and Spencer has his face resting on the top of my seat, his cheek is inches away from my face, and I can see the 5 o'clock shadow he has growing in. My hand twitches in my lap, and I have to force myself not to reach up and stroke his cheek. I love running my hands through a man's scruff, and my fingers are itching to touch him.

"Did you hear me?" Spencer's breath smells like peppermint, which goes nicely with the rest of him smelling like a freaking Christmas tree. "Phoebe?"

"What, sorry. I was zoning out. What did you say?" I feel the blood rush to my cheeks as he flashes that stupid smile again. There's no way I don't look like a full-faced tomato right now.

"I asked how you were enjoying living in New York. I've always wanted to visit," he says.

Honestly, I hate living in New York. The city is crowded, the traffic is horrible, and it takes forever to get anywhere. But, I fought my parents so hard when I got accepted into NYU to study art history. They wanted me to stay closer to home since Piper was leaving for basic training after graduation and could get stationed anywhere in the world. I didn't think it was fair to have to be the one to pick up the emotional slack for everyone when all I wanted to do was branch out and experience life outside of this small town.

How stupid and naive I was.

But I don't tell him any of that because that would be admitting failure, and I'm not down for that. Especially because I don't know how to break the news to my family that I've realized that working in the museum isn't everything I hoped it would be and that I'm toying around with the idea of returning to school to get a teaching degree. I'll save that drama and disappointment for another day, though.

Instead, I give Spencer the answer everyone expects. "I love it. The city at night is beautiful, and there's nothing quite as remarkable as New Year's Eve at Times Square,"

I'm not lying about that second part. I went by myself on New Year's after I moved to the city. It was even better in person than it is on the television. Everyone is lost in the moment of bliss and excitement while they scream out the numbers as the clock runs down. The lights, the snow cascading gently onto the crowd, the applause—it's one of the better moments I've experienced while living there.

It was also one of the most lonely.

Piper pulls into the driveway of our childhood home, and I'm hit with a wave of homesickness that makes my chest feel tight and heavy. I stare at all the Christmas lights strung up perfectly around the A-frame of the blue house and all the same decorations that have covered our yard and patio for my entire life. Seeing the giant Christmas tree in the big bay window at the front of the house—it's all the same. Exactly the way it was when I left five years ago. I have to choke back a sob that's trying to claw its way out of my throat. I've missed this place so much.

Piper reaches over and squeezes my hand twice. She must know I'm on the verge of losing it because two squeezes have always been our silent code when words fail us. Two squeezes mean, 'Are you okay?'. Three squeezes means 'I will be'.

I squeeze her hand back three times and give her a sad smile. I know she has to miss this place even more than I do. She's half a world away at all times.

"Okay, let's take this food inside before this turns into some weird crying fest thing," Spencer says from the backseat. I let out a small laugh before remembering I dislike him.

Ha. As if telling myself that can make it true.

We grab the food and head up the front steps to the house when I see something move from above us. I take a few steps back to better view the second-story windows and slip on the step, falling backward into the yard.

The breath is knocked out of me, and I'm pretty sure my entire body is bruised from behind. Piper is laughing like a hyena and jumping up and down on the porch *while* pointing her phone at me. I'm going to kill her as soon as I can force my body to work again.

I start to sit up slowly when Spencer steps forward and reaches his hand out to help me up. When our hands touch, I feel like an electric current flows through my entire body. I suck in a startled breath at the same time he does. He hoists me up and out of the snow, and I stumble directly into his arms.

His very warm, very muscled arms.

I must not fall for Spencer Larson.

I will not fall for Spencer Larson.

I cannot fall for Spencer freaking Larson.

Repeating my mantra helps me take that much-needed step out of his arms, and I look up into his eyes. "Thank you," I tell him with a polite smile. I'm glad it's dark enough now that he can't see how red my face is.

"You're welcome," he answers softly, smiling a crooked smile back down at me. This smile isn't the panty-dropping smile I've gotten used to over the last hour of being around him. This one is more reserved and softer somehow. This smile feels significantly more intimate and, strangely, like it was made just for me.

Something moves and catches my eye again before I can say anything back to him. I narrow my eyes and look at Piper.

"Why is there a cat in my bedroom window?"

"Oh, don't mind him. That's just Little E," Piper answers with a shrug before walking back up the steps to the front door. "Dad decided that this whole empty nest thing was for the birds after Phil moved out, so he got himself a stray."

Okay, maybe things aren't exactly the same as when I left. I didn't know that my little brother moved out. I guess I haven't been the best daughter or sister. I don't remember the last time I answered my parent's phone calls without trying to rush through the conversation. And I can't count how many unanswered texts Phillip has sent me over the last few months.

I look back up at the cat who has replaced me, and I feel a lump in my throat as I follow Piper and Spencer into the house. I'm hit with a wave of sadness as I realize just how much I've missed since I've been gone.

CHAPTER SIX

Spencer

We're all crammed in tight around the Andrews' family table, much like we used to when we were all kids. The pizza has been demolished, and the pasta and breadsticks are nearly empty. I'm not sure where Austin and Phil ran off with the brownies, but I'll be sure to hunt them down before I leave because Lucene's brownies are the best brownies on the entire planet.

Dad and Mr. Andrews are in the den watching whatever sport is playing, and Mrs. Andrews and Mom got up a few minutes ago to start cleaning up the dishes. Piper is outside on the back porch, all bundled up in her winter coat and beanie, talking on the phone with a friend of hers back in Germany.

That just leaves Phoebe and I at the table.

I haven't been able to stop sneaking peeks at her all night. Something is bothering her, and it's bothering me that I don't know what it is. Ever since we pulled up to her house, she's seemed off. It's like an aura of sadness surrounds her. When we got inside with the food, everyone did their usual song and dance with lots of hugs and even more 'We've missed yous,' but the fire in Phoebe's eyes had completely smoldered out. A normal person would just be able to reach out and ask if she's okay, but I know I'm the last person in this house she'd feel comfortable opening up to.

My eyes follow her as she stands up and walks towards the front door. A moment later, I hear that tell-tale sound of a sniffle right before the front door opens and closes.

I'm pretty sure she's crying. And like the giant idiot that I am, I stand up and follow her outside. I can't just let her sneak away and cry alone. Not when it's evident that something is upsetting her.

How am I the only one to see how sad she is?

Her family surrounds us, yet nobody seems to really *see* her. That bothers me a lot more than it should. I will check if she's okay, and then I'll let her be.

At least, that's what I keep telling myself.

I grab my coat, quietly open the front door, and close it behind me. When I turn, I see her sitting on the front steps. Her arms are wrapped around her knees, pulled tightly to her chest. The Christmas lights on the house illuminate her face just enough to see the tears glistening on her cheeks. All I want to do is hold her until she stops crying.

Instead, I take a loud enough step towards her so she knows I'm here. I don't want to startle her and upset her even more. She turns her face in my direction and quickly wipes the evidence of her distress off with the back of her hands. Her mascara smears slightly on the corners of her eyes, but somehow, it makes her even more beautiful.

She hasn't told me to leave, so I take that as permission to get closer to her. As I do, I place my jacket over her shoulders. Then, I sit down a respectful distance from the step next to her.

She shrugs my jacket and pulls it tight against her before turning towards me. "Thanks," she says, her voice hoarse from crying.

"You're welcome," I answer back softly. "I know it's stupid to ask if you're alright, so I won't. But I'm here if you want to talk about it." I raise my hands like I'm offering up a peace treaty between us. "I promise no fighting, no questions, and I'll only offer advice if you want me to. You can just let this be an old-fashioned bitch-session."

She huffs out a shaky laugh and wipes at her eyes again. "You must talk to my dad a lot," she replies. "Because he is the only person I've ever met that uses the term 'old-fashioned bitch-session'." She lets out another small laugh and then smiles at me.

Her smile is brighter and infinitely more stunning than the Christmas lights hanging above us. I wish I could spend the rest of my life keeping that smile on her face.

"Honestly, I feel stupid for crying," she utters. "I guess I just forgot how much I missed being home. Five years ago, I couldn't wait to escape this town and get as far away from my family as possible." She pulls my coat tighter around herself before she continues. "And I know how selfish that must sound because my family is amazing. Like truly, the best family I could've ever asked for. But I couldn't wait to put this life behind me."

It takes every ounce of restraint not to scoot closer to her and put my arm around her as she starts crying again. I know exactly how she feels because I've done the whole run away from home thing, and when I came back, I realized how stupid I had been. I moved back home two weeks after graduating with my teaching degree and haven't regretted that for a second.

She wipes angrily at her face this time. "I didn't think I missed being here so much until we pulled up to the house and saw that stupid cat in my bedroom window. It doesn't even feel like my bedroom window anymore! I've been so wrapped up trying to force myself to be happy in the big city that I've missed everything back home. I didn't even know Phillip had moved out until about an hour ago because I had never asked. I've been avoiding my family for years. And for what? What type of person gets up and leaves home and then never calls to check on anyone?" She throws her head into her hands and lets out a gut-wrenching sob.

This time, I can't stop myself from scooting closer and pulling her into my arms. I don't care if she hates me. I can't stand the idea of her hurting this badly on the inside and being left alone to suffer through these feelings. She cries huge, body-wracking sobs into my chest, and I hold her tighter. She may feel like she's falling apart, but I'll do whatever I can to keep her from entirely breaking.

"It makes you human, Phoebe. I don't know a single kid who can't wait to fly away from the nest when it's time," I tell her, rubbing soft circles on her back. "Well, except maybe Austin and Phil. They were forced to fly. And they didn't get very far."

"What do you mean?"

"They are rooming together in the apartments across the street from the community college. They just moved last week, so it doesn't make you a bad sister for not knowing that. Austin didn't even tell me until yesterday," I chuckle. "You know those two live in a world of their own."

I feel her body shake with laughter. "And my dad got a cat that fast?" Phoebe asks.

"Well, sort of, but not really." She pulls back and furrows her brows in confusion as she looks at me. "Okay, that cat has been hanging out on this street for several months. He just mosied from house to house until someone let him in. Your dad just happened to be that someone. And it was more like an accidental adoption. Word has it, that cat had been hiding in your house for a few days before your mom found him taking a dump in the bathtub."

"No, she didn't!" Phoebe shouts out before covering her mouth.

"Yep. Linda tried to kick the cat out. She even called my mom to help. But your dad came home as they tried to wrestle him into a box, and that demon cat jumped out and climbed right up Ed's leg. He claimed that cat was his and named him Enrique after some kickboxer from back in the day. He said he had the heart of a fighter and could stay."

"This sounds like something Dad would do. I wish I were here to see the expression on Mom's face when she caught that cat in the tub." She pulls away from me to where we sit side by side but keeps her body pressed against mine. "Thank you. Again," she says as she brushes away a loose strand of red hair that's fallen in front of her eyes. "For the jacket and letting me get all that out."

"You're welcome, Pheebs."

We're both silent for a few minutes before the door opens loudly behind us, causing Phoebe to jump off the step and move as far away from me as she can. My pride takes a minor offense to that, but I'm also basking in happiness. She didn't push me away when I first came out to check on her. And she let me comfort her. I never imagined a moment like this with her in the last few years. That blossom of hope swells in my stomach.

"Hey, Phil. What's up?" Phoebe says with a relaxed and calm demeanor. Nobody would believe me if I told them she had been crying in my arms sixty seconds ago. It's awe-inspiring and a little terrifying that she can flip a switch that fast.

Phillip looks back and forth at us, and I swear he gets a little mischievous twinkle in his eyes like he's planning one of his stupid pranks. I glare at him and shake my head in a firm 'no.' I don't know what he's planning, but he better leave his sister alone for now. He smirks at me before focusing on Phoebe.

"Family meeting time. The 'rents want to talk to all of us," he tells her.

She starts following him inside, and I take that as my cue to leave. I head to my parent's house, which is conveniently just across the street, when Phillip calls me after me.

"You too, Larson. It's a multi-family meeting."

Phoebe turns around and looks at me with a confused expression that matches mine. We haven't had a multi-family meeting in years. I shrug my shoulders at her before following her inside. Might as well see what all the fuss is about.

Chapter seven

Phoebe

I'm mortified as Spencer follows me into the house. I can't believe I let any of that happen. But worse, I can't believe I enjoyed every minute of it. I'm obviously still attracted to the man. How could I not be when he grew up to look like, well, an even sexier Clark Kent? Minus the wide-rimmed glasses. However, he'd probably look sexy in those, too.

"Pheebs, hunny. Sit here next to me. I feel like I've hardly had a moment with you since you got here," Mom says and pats the unoccupied chair beside her. I graciously take her up on her offer, and as soon as I'm seated, she wraps her arms around me and kisses me on my forehead.

"I missed you, Mama. Thanks for having me at the last minute."

"Oh, hush. You know this house will forever be your home. We're so happy you were able to make it. I know your life is busy in the big city, but I'm so happy you came home for Christmas this year." I hug her back tightly and we both share teary smiles. I don't know how I'm going to leave here. I could stay wrapped in my mom's arms for the rest of my life and be content.

Dad stands at the head of the table, and we all give him our full attention. When Dad stands up during a family meeting, it means business. He clears his throat loudly and prepares to begin his speech—because there's always a speech.

"Alright, first off, thank you all for being here. I know it's not easy to travel so far for the holidays." He winks at Piper and me and gets a laugh out of most of the table. "I can't remember the last time our families could sit down at this table and not have an empty chair. Mary, John, thank you for making time to get yourselves and your rowdy boys here tonight." He tips his head at Spencer and Austin, then reaches down to pick up something at his feet.

When he comes up, I see that he has the cat in his arms, and I have to fight my eyeballs from trying to roll into the back of my skull when I notice that Dad and Little E have matching red sweaters. He lifts the cat into a position that looks like he's trying to rock a baby to sleep and then starts baby-talking to this cat as he repeatedly pets his fuzzy little head.

"Everyone say hi to Little E."

If there were crickets in the room, they'd be chirping amidst the awkward silence that follows that request.

"Baby, why don't you continue? It's getting late, and I'm sure the girls are tired from traveling," Mom suggests.

"No, not until everyone says hi to Little E," he presses.

Piper and I make eye contact, and she rolls her eyes and sighs loudly. We both tell Little E hi, which earns us a smile from Dad. I can't believe I left for a few years and returned to Mr. Cat Dad. We weren't allowed any pets growing up except for fish, which kept going belly up on us.

The rest of the table greets Little E with a very unenthusiastic hello. As soon as they do, he scampers out of Dad's arms and runs up the stairs like the little demon child he is.

Dad claps his hands together loudly and finally retakes a seat.

"Okay, so. We oldies thought since it's the first Christmas that you've all been home together in years, we should make it an extra fun one. Mary, can you grab the box?"

Mary stands up quickly and claps her hands in a giddy way. She grabs a small box from the mantle and hands it to Dad. She ruffles Austin's and Phil's hair, which earns her shouts of protest from both of them before taking her seat again.

"In this box, there are five tasks," Dad explains, and I think we all know exactly what's going on now. Piper starts jumping up and down in her seat like an excited child while Austin and Phillip are high-fiving each other with wicked smiles. I look across the table, and my eyes meet Spencer's. He has an amused expression tugging on the corner of his lips, and I feel my own trying to fight its way out.

John and Mom are both smiling widely now, and Mary is downright ecstatic as Dad starts to explain the rules of the game.

The same game we played for many years as children.

The Mistletoe Feud.

I feel myself start to get antsy. I've *never* won The Mistletoe Feud, but that changes this year. I'm older, wiser, and ready to pull out all the stops to win.

That crown will be mine this time.

"Ahh, hell with it." Dad throws his hands up in defeat and pushes the box towards Piper. "Linda printed the rules this year, and you can read them. My old man eyes don't work the way they used to."

"Dad, you're not even sixty yet." Phillip gripes as Piper stands up to pass around the small paper squares to all of us 'children.'

"When you get to be my age—"

"Oh my gosh. Please don't turn this into one of those 'back in my day I had to hike through the snow for five miles to and from school' talks," Piper hassles him, earning a gruff but amused laugh from Dad. She hands me my rule sheet, and I gaze down at it, knowing precisely what it's going to say but enjoying the familiarity of it. It's quite comforting knowing that some things won't change, even if I never expected to play this silly game again.

THE MISTLETOE FEUD 2023

Goal: To win the most challenges and be crowned the Mistletoe King or Queen

Players: Spencer Larson, Piper Andrews, Phoebe Andrews, Austin Larson, Phillip Andrews

Judges: Ed and Linda Andrews // John and Mary Larson

Rules: Every day the group will be assigned a task. Nobody will know before what task it will be, so don't try to pester the oldies.
Cheaters WILL NOT win.
You will have from 11:00 AM until 6:00 PM to successfully complete your tasks and show them to the judges. You do not have to stay in the house to do each task, but you will need to be back for the judging of the daily challenge no later than 6:00 PM. If you fail to show up on time, you will be eliminated from that challenge.
The winner will be selected based on whoever completes the task with the most festive flair.
Each winner will be written on the scoreboard hanging above the mantle at the Andrews' house. Whomever has the most wins by the end of the five days will be crowned the winner of The Mistletoe Feud and win the title of Mistletoe King or Queen.

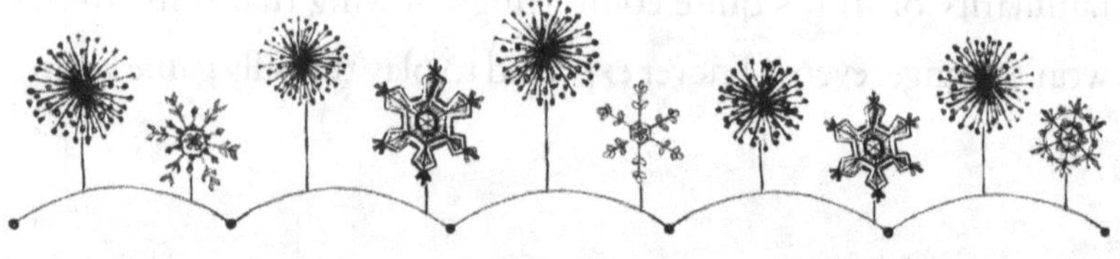

Okay, maybe these rules aren't exactly the same as they were when we were younger, but that makes me feel even more competitive. I'm really want to win this thing. I know I sound like a petulant child, but Pipes has never let me forget how many times she's won over the years.

Spoiler alert: she's won more times than any of us have.

Now, I feel like I have a really good shot at winning because back then, we weren't allowed to leave the house to complete our challenges. Do you know how difficult it is for five of us to try to bake cookies using one oven? It was impossible. By the time I finally got to use the oven, I didn't have enough time to cool my cookies. Nothing screams 'winner' like the tragic melted faces of my gingerbread men cookies.

The room is quiet except for the crackle of the log burning in the fireplace as we read the newly amended rule sheet. I mentally start thinking of what tasks our parents must have for us. Every year, they had different tasks, but they were all holiday-themed, and they obviously had to be kid-friendly back then. Let's see: there was the cookie decorating contest, the ugly sweaters, the snowman, gift wrapping, and gingerbread houses. What else?

"Are you trying to remember what tasks they gave us?" I let out a shrill yelp and nearly jump out of my skin when I realize Phillip is sitting beside me. My eyes widen as I scan the room and notice the entire table is empty except for him and Spencer. I must have really been spacing out this time because I don't remember seeing anyone stand up and leave. I was too focused on plotting.

"Yeah, I am. Want to help?" I smile at my brother fondly. He's grown up so much since I saw him in New York last Christmas. I keep reminding myself that my baby brother is a full-fledged adult now. Whatever that means for *him*.

"What, no! I can't help you win!"

"You owe me for that Taylor Swift video you snuck of me last Christmas." My fond smile quickly turns into a cocky one as I narrow my eyes at him. I know he'll help now that I've called him out on his shenanigans.

"What Taylor Swift video?" Spencer asks from across the table. I feel my cheeks turning red, and I shake my head at Phillip when he pulls his phone out of his back pocket. He smirks, and I pinch his leg hard under the table.

"I swear I will murder you, Phillip," I seethe under my breath at him. He dares to wink at me before he turns his attention to Spencer.

"Oh, it's nothing, really," Phil tells Spencer. "I just got this great video of Pheebs singing her heart out to some Swiftie song in the shower after Kevin dumped her last Christmas."

I close my eyes and focus on steadying my breathing. I don't want to talk about this. And I definitely don't want Spencer to know about it. He doesn't get to know that another stupid man has broken my douchebag-loving heart.

When I open my eyes, I find him staring at me from across the table with a strange expression. I almost ask him what's wrong, but he breaks eye contact with me and looks at Phil.

"So you mean to tell me you snuck into the bathroom while your sister was butt naked and recorded her?" he asks Phil, his face completely deadpan.

"Oh, what the—no! I wasn't in the bathroom with her! I was outside the door," Phil yells and stands to leave. He's a very hot-headed little dude—even if he's now a foot taller than me.

"Well, then, how do you know it was Phoebe? She could have just had some crappy YouTuber singing and couldn't reach her phone to change it," Spencer argues.

Whenever I think I'm talking myself out of falling for him again, he does something swoon-worthy like that. I could kiss the man just for skipping over the whole breakup part of Phil's story altogether. Even if he sort of just admitted that I have a crappy singing voice.

"It was her! I know what my sister sounds like when she sings."

I have to hold back a laugh when I see how red Phil's face is getting. Like I said, hot-headed.

"No, Spencer's right. It was just a video ad. I don't even like her music," I say nonchalantly with a shrug. I catch Spencer's gaze again, and he's trying so hard not to laugh, which makes me want to laugh.

When did we become a tolerable unit?

"Urg! You two are still just as annoying as you were five years ago. I'm leaving now. I'll see you two tomorrow to wipe those smiles off your faces when I win the first task."

"I love you, turd face!" I yell out to him right after he stalks out of the room.

He pops his head back into the dining room, and I know I'm forgiven when I see the twinkle in his green eyes. "I love you too, turd head. I'm glad you're home. Also, everybody loves our girl T. Swift. You don't have to lie to save face in front of *him*." He shoots a glare Spencer's way before he turns on his heel and leaves again.

"Turd head?" Spencer is looking at me with an amused look on his face.

"He's called me that for as long as I can remember," I answer him with a soft laugh. "I called him a turd face once for stealing the last cookie, and in response, he called me a turd head and gave me half. It's just always been our thing."

Spencer smiles at me and gets to his feet. "I'll see you tomorrow, Pheebs."

I don't answer him back. Instead, I'm stuck on mute, watching him walk away and enjoy every second.

That man sure has an ass on him.

CHAPTER EIGHT

Spencer

I'm walking up the steps to the Andrews' house with an extra large and extra strong black coffee in one hand and a box of dozen holiday-themed donuts in the other. I slept horribly last night—tossing and turning all night in a restless sleep. All I kept thinking about was how excited I was to wake up and see Phoebe again.

Which, in hindsight, I know, is a foolish thing to get my hopes up for. Yes, Phoebe may have given me a solid ten minutes of her attention last night without it turning ugly, but I don't for one-second think that it's going to be repeated.

She still doesn't know the whole story of what went on between her sister and me all those years ago, and it's *not* something I can tell her. That truth will always be up to Piper to tell, and I will silently bear that weight until she's ready to because that's what friends do for each other. Piper and I may not have talked over the last few years, but I'll always consider her one of my best friends. I may be not-so-silently crushing on her sister, but I'll never betray her trust to get another shot at being with Phoebe.

I ring the doorbell with my elbow, and a moment later, Piper answers the door with a broad smile. Her hair is pushed back with one of those bandana things. It has a candy cane design, and she has little reindeer earrings dangling from her ears.

"Oh my gosh, Spence! You're officially back to best friend status," she exclaims excitedly, snatching the box of donuts out of my hands before turning on her Grinch-slippered heel back into the house.

"Good morning to you too, Pipes," I mutter under my breath with a laugh and follow her into the house, closing the door softly behind me.

It's only 9:40 in the morning, but Mrs. Andrews has the whole house in disarray. There are rolls of wrapping paper thrown haphazardly in every direction, along with rolls of tape and ribbons of every color. I spy Little E in the living room sizing up the giant tree sitting in front of the bay window like he's trying to figure out how to climb it without knocking every ornament down on his way up. He's wearing another sweater today, and this one is green with little Christmas trees all over it. I'm sure Mr. Andrews is wearing a very similar one.

Both of my parents are sitting at the kitchen table with mugs of coffee in their hands, so I make my way over there to say hello. I don't live far from here—only about a twenty-minute drive to my small cabin. It's at the base of the Appalachian Mountains that run through our small town of Noelsville, North Carolina. I love being close enough to see my family whenever I want.

I kiss my mom on the cheek before I clap my dad on the shoulder. "I brought donuts from Adalene's Bakery. I don't know where Piper is hiding them, though," I tell them as I sit across from them.

"I'm sure she has inhaled half the box already," Phoebe says from behind me with a laugh. I freeze when I hear her voice. How does just hearing the sound of her voice turn me into this panic-riddled shell of a man? My heart is trying to pound out of my chest, and my palms go clammy within seconds of her entering the room. I quickly wipe them on my jeans before standing up and pulling a chair for her.

A chair conveniently next to me because I'm a masochist and love to torture myself even further.

I don't look at her as she quickly thanks me before taking a seat. I do, however, make eye contact with my mom from across the table, and she looks like she's about to combust in pure joy. She has never been quiet about the fact that she'd love me and Phoebe to get together one day, but she doesn't have all the facts of our sordid past. I'm not going to share them with her. So instead, I'll endure the excited glances and winks she keeps not-so-subtly throwing my way.

The front door opens loudly from behind us, and I hear both my brother and Phillip laughing loudly about something as they parade into the dining room to join us. Piper comes running in behind them with the box of donuts in her hands. She places the box down in the middle of the table, and Dad is the first to snatch it. When he opens it, I'm surprised to see that Piper hasn't touched any of them.

Surprised—and wary.

Our brothers got their knack for pranks and learned their tricks from someone, and it wasn't me.

Dad inspects the donuts quietly before grabbing a chocolate-glazed one covered in red and green sprinkles and hands it to Mom. I've always admired how Dad always puts Mom first, whether it's the first donut from the box or the first mug of coffee from the freshly brewed pot. He's always taken care of her needs before his own. They smile at each other with a timeless sort of affection, and she grabs one of the sugar donuts from the box for Dad before sliding the box across the table to Phoebe. She declines a donut and slides the box over to Phillip and Austin.

They both take no time grabbing two of the Christmas-decorated ones. One is bright green with a tree on it, and the other has chocolate and is decorated with little strings of Christmas lights using large colored sprinkles. I look over and see Piper walking back into the dining room. She leans against the doorway, laughing silently and winking at her sister. I turn back to see Phoebe pull out her phone next to me.

A few seconds later, the boys spit their donuts into their napkins and yell like hyenas. Phoebe and Piper start laughing hysterically. I look back and forth between the four of them in confusion.

"What did I just miss?" Mrs. Andrews says as she strolls into the dining room with Mr. Andrews following hot on her heels.

His sweater definitely matches Little E's. They both have amused smiles painted on their faces as they take in the scene.

"Piper put toothpaste in the donuts!" Phillip yells out loudly. He's trying to wipe his tongue off with the napkins while Austin grabs his donut and runs into the kitchen. I can't contain the laugh that bubbles out of my throat when I hear the sink turn on and the distinct sound of a gargle.

Phoebe stands and hands Piper her phone. They give each other a high five before returning to the table and grabbing donuts for themselves.

"Are the rest of the donuts safe?" Mr. Andrews asks as he peers skeptically into the box.

Piper pulls the box towards her. "Yep, the rest are spearmint free!" She blows Phil a kiss as he glares at her from across the table. I can see the bright green toothpaste oozing from his discarded donut.

Austin comes back and sits down without saying a word. I'm sure he's already plotting his revenge. Philip may be the hothead, but Austin is the real danger. He's too smart for his own good and always at least five steps ahead when pranking one of us.

"You know they'll get you back for this, right?" I look at both Phoebe and Piper and shake my head at them when they smile wider. They may be identical twins, but their smiles couldn't be more different. Phoebe keeps her lips together when she smiles, making her look soft and gentle. Piper's smile is big and wide enough to show off every tooth in her mouth.

"Are we all done messing around? Or do you all want to get eliminated for the first round?" Mr. Andrews asks in a no-non-sense tone.

We all hush up quickly and give him our full attention. Who would have thought that all of us would still be this excited about this game years into our adulthood?

"Linda, dear, can you grab the box?"

We all watch as Mrs. Andrews stands and grabs a box from under the tree. It's similar to the box from last night, but this one is much larger.

Mr. Andrews stands up and puts his reading glasses on before taking the box from his wife. "Who wants to open the first task?"

Everyone but Phoebe and I yell. I peek at her and see that she has her serious face on. I could always tell when she was in the zone because she had the most intense and 'in it to win it' expression.

"I flew across the ocean to be here; I should get dibs on opening the first box!" Piper shouts while tossing a look of irritation at Phil before he can speak a single word.

"Yes, I think that's fair," Mom agrees with her, earning a giant smile from Piper in return.

Mr. Andrews slides the box over to Piper, and we all wait in muted anticipation to see what this first task will be. It feels like we're ten years old again, waiting to hear the task before darting off quickly to opposite ends of the house.

Piper unwraps the box, tugs the lid off, pulls a small piece of paper out, and starts to read it. Phoebe stands up to get a better look at what's inside, and her eyes widen for a fraction of a second before she sits back down. Now I'm even more curious about what our parents have been up to.

"What's it say?" Austin begs from his end of the table.

Piper shoots him a look of annoyance, then reads us the first task.

TASK ONE

In this box there are five different aprons.
Each of you will pull an apron blindly from the box.
Every apron has a logo and job attached to it, which will
get you into the town's Christmas Market and lead you to
your assigned booth for the day.
Whoever sells the most items from their booth will be the
winner for the first task.
Make sure to be back by 6:00 PM with proof of items sold!
Have fun, and good luck!

Piper closes her eyes, pulls a red apron from the box, and then slides it over to Phoebe. She follows suit. Her apron is green with red polka dots, and she passes the box to me. I look at the ceiling, reach blindly into the box, pull my apron out, and then slide the box over to Phil and Austin. I peer down at the apron I pulled out. It's brown with little green trees, and the logo says "Buck's Christmas Tree Farm."

"I guess you're stuck working the tree tent," Phoebe says as she peers at my apron.

"What did you get?"

"I'll be beating all of you this time," she answers back with a cocky grin. "Because I'll be working at Nana's Gingerbread House." She proudly holds up her apron, and Phil groans from across the table.

"She's totally going to beat us," he says in defeat, holding his bright yellow apron up. "I got Santa's Eggnog Hut. Nobody even likes eggnog."

"Hey, I love eggnog!" Mr. Andrews flashes us all a smile.

"Okay, I'll take that back. Only the oldies will come and buy some because everyone under the age of 30 knows that eggnog is disgusting," Phillip quips back.

"What did you get, honey?" Mrs. Andrews asks Piper.

"I'll be selling copious amounts of fudge at Terry's Fudge Shop." She smiles brightly at her mom. Phoebe lets out a small groan of distress beside me.

Everyone at the Christmas Market goes ham over Terry's fudge, and most people buy it by the pound to save for later since he only makes it during the holidays.

"You guys can all suck it when I come in with the uncontested win," Austin boasts. "Nobody leaves the market without buying a wooden engraved ornament by Conrad at Conrad's Rad Ornaments."

"Crap," Phoebe mutters in defeat as we all stand and get ready to head over to the market. Her shoulders are already sagging with disappointment.

Somehow, someway, I'm going to make sure she wins this thing.

CHAPTER NINE

Phoebe

"Come and get your freshly baked gingerbread cookies!" I yell for what feels like the hundredth time. My booth is near the front of the market, so I can try to get as many newcomers as possible as soon as they enter the town square. So far, I've sold 17 cookies, and I've only been here for 45 minutes. I wish I could take a quick break to peep at the competition, but Nana would side-eye me so hard, and I sort of wilt under her death stare. For a lady who bakes the cutest little gingerbread men and women, she's pretty cutthroat. She reminds me a lot of Mrs. Jones from the library back in New York.

But my goodness, she makes the best cookies. And they smell *so* good. If I could bottle this smell, I'd cover my body with it 24/7. I bet a certain tall and handsome competitor would happily lick it off...

"Drooling on the job, Pheebs?"

Speak of the devil.

I see Spencer walking by my booth with a giant Christmas tree slung effortlessly over his shoulder. His biceps are bulging out of the sleeves of his rolled-up blue flannel. The brown apron is wrapped snugly across that broad chest of his, and I have to physically wipe away the drool that's about to drip out of my mouth when I see that he has his hat on backward. How on earth does he make the backward hat thing look so sexy?

"How many trees have you sold?"

"This is my first one, actually," he answers before stopping next to my booth and propping the tree against the side. "How many cookies have you sold?" he asks me as he takes the bottom of his apron and uses it to wipe the sweat off his face. It's not a warm day, but I guess towing heavy trees to the parking lot for customers is a sweaty job—not that I'm minding the view.

Wait, how has he only sold one tree? I swear I've seen multiple people walk by, pulling their trees in the little red and green wagons the tree farm provides.

"You're not lying to me about how many you've sold, are you?" I cock my eyebrow at him and take a bite of my fourth gingerbread cookie. Perk of this booth, Nana gives me all the cookies I want as long as I watch the register so she doesn't have to.

He tugs his hat off and brushes a hand through his sandy blond hair before putting his hat back in place. "Why would I lie about that, Phoebe?"

The way he says my name makes me feel giddy inside. What is wrong with me? I cannot let myself fall for him again...not after he kissed Piper.

But there's nothing wrong with admiring him. Maybe I could let him become a friend again? There's nothing wrong with that, right? He was so sweet last night during my minor breakdown, and I *could* use a friend.

He's still standing there looking like a Greek God when another customer walks up. I give Spencer a small smile and turn my attention to the person standing at the counter.

And then my whole stomach falls out of my ass because the man standing in front of me is Kevin.

The man that never spoke to me again after last Christmas Eve.

The man who broke my heart last year and dumped me in front of my family.

The man who told me to leave and never gave me a reason why.

That man is standing at my booth, and he's *smiling* at me.

"Hey there, gorgeous," Kevin coos as he beams at me like he didn't rip my heart out and smash it into a billion and one pieces last year.

The smile I had plastered on my face about two seconds ago turns into a scowl immediately. "What are you doing here, Kevin?" I step away from the counter and cross my arms across my chest. It might seem like a petulant move, but it makes me feel like I'm wearing armor while guarding my heart.

"I wanted to talk to you, and you refuse to answer my calls."

"Why would I bother answering your calls a year *after* you dumped me and ghosted me?" I snap back.

"That was unkind of me. And I'm here to talk about it," Kevin sighs and runs his hand through his dark hair. "I just want to talk. Please?"

I feel my resolve melting away slowly, like the poor faces of the gingerbread men I tried to bake myself years ago. Whether I like it or not, I've always wondered why he left me. He gave me no reason and absolutely no closure. My heart's been closed off and guarded ever since, and I'd really love it if I could attempt to open it up again.

I glance over to where Spencer is standing, and my heart drops when I see that he's gone. I didn't even notice him walk away, but his giant tree is missing, too. I wish he were here now for that same emotional support he lent me last night.

I look back over to Kevin, who is standing there looking like he just stepped out of a GQ magazine. His dark hair is in a stylish disarray that only he can pull off, and his dark eyes are still that same smug chocolate brown with hints of gold in them. The jeans he's wearing look brand new and freshly pressed to go right along with his taupe overcoat and deep green scarf. It's honestly alarming how good-looking he is, and it's so unfair. He doesn't look like he's spent the last year crying himself to sleep while wondering if there's a way to change every piece of you to make someone love you enough to stay.

To choose *you.*

"Okay," I finally answer him. "You can get one minute of conversation for every cookie you buy." I cock my eyebrow at him and wave my hand toward the delicious assortment of cookies on the counter between us.

Kevin smiles as he steps closer to get a better look at them. His expensive cologne wafts over me. I'm momentarily taken back to all the nights we spent tangled up in bed together, both of us basking in the New York sunrise peeking through the open blinds of his home, surrounded by that same cologne.

"I'll take sixty cookies then," he says smugly. Money has never been an issue for him, but this is ridiculous.

"I'm not letting you buy sixty cookies, Kevin." I throw my hands up in defeat. "Just tell me what you want to tell me so I can return to winning."

"What are you winning?"

"Uh, umm. It's nothing," I stammer out. I'm not about to tell Kevin I'm competing in my family's childhood game and that I'm very much in it to win it. He never understood the juvenile things in life, like having a Gizmo backpack just for fun. That was too *immature* for his eclectic tastes.

"Look at you blushing for me, Phoebe. Don't you miss this? Don't you miss us?" he preens as he steps closer to the counter—to me.

I take an unsettled step back. Because part of me does miss him, and another part of me wants to spit in his face and scream at him to leave me alone.

Do I miss *him* necessarily? Or do I miss not being alone? Because this last year has been nothing but my own personal hell of loneliness.

"Hey babe, how's work going?" I feel an arm sneak around my waist, and the smell of Christmas trees surrounds me.

Spencer.

I gaze up at him, and he's looking at Kevin with his panty-dropper smile plastered all over his face. He squeezes me against him tighter. I know I should be pushing him away, but the look of envy on Kevin's face keeps me from doing just that.

"Hi, hun! I was wondering when you'd get here." I let my gaze linger on Kevin momentarily before smiling at Spencer. My stomach goes haywire when his eyes meet mine, and he flashes that soft, crooked smile—the smile I've secretly reserved as my own.

Spencer reaches out over the counter, and Kevin stumbles forward to shake his hand in return. "Hi, I'm Spencer. Phoebe's boyfriend. Did I hear that you wanted to buy sixty cookies?"

"I, uh. Yeah. I'm Kevin," he responds curtly and pulls out his wallet. His eyes don't leave Spencer's while he hands me his credit card.

"Thanks, Kevin. I'll have these boxed up for you in a jiffy!" I pull out of Spencer's grasp and start counting cookies. I feel the testosterone building next to me, but I refuse to acknowledge it. I'm still reeling that Spencer came to my rescue—again.

And I might be freaking out over the butterflies that have taken flight in my stomach over the fact that Spencer *freaking* Larson called himself my boyfriend.

Get a grip, Pheebs. He's just playing nice because he saw you again floundering in Kevin's presence. No matter how handsome and sweet he may seem now, he's still the same guy who kissed Piper on our first date.

I finish packaging the cookies and place the extra large bag between us on the counter. "Don't eat them all at once. Nobody wants a stomach ache during Christmas," I joke. They both give me small smiles full of pity for the lame joke. I feel like I'm in some twisted twilight zone with the two of them together. Never in a million years did I expect these two ever to cross paths. I can't say this whole 'both guys that broke my heart during the holidays would be hanging out together as I sold cookies' was ever on my bingo card.

"Can I talk to you later?" Kevin asks quietly as he grabs the bag. He glances over at Spencer before he gets closer to me. "Please?"

I can't help but feel a slight twinge in my gut that makes me feel sorry for him. Which I know is stupid, as he dumped me. But I loved him once, and I think that alone deserves five minutes of my time.

"Yeah, I'll text you," I tell him. "See you later, Kev."

He smiles and gives Spencer a quick nod before walking away from the booth and into the market. I watch him until he entirely disappears into the crowd and out of view. I turn to Spencer to thank him for making this weird situation a lot more bizarre but a lot less stressful.

"Good luck selling the rest of these cookies. I gotta go sell more trees if I want a shot at winning this one," Spencer says before giving me a wave and walking off.

I'm pretty sure my mouth is still hanging open as he disappears into the crowd himself.

What in the world just happened?

CHAPTER TEN

Spencer

It's official. I'm the biggest idiot ever to walk the streets of Noelsville. I've been replaying the whole scene all day long in my mind.

Phoebe and Kevin.

Kevin with Phoebe.

Seeing them together, smiling together—I hated every moment of it. I knew the second that his fancy coat-wearing self walked up that he was someone from her past. She didn't look thrilled to see him, which I didn't mind. But when she didn't immediately send him away—and the pet names—I couldn't stand there and listen to them.

So I left and took the giant seven-foot tree to the customer's car while she kept shopping at the market. When I came back, I just happened to walk right past Phoebe's booth, and my traitorous eyes couldn't *not* look over at her. How could I not? She's always been beautiful, but today, there was a glow about her that's been missing since she got back to town. I don't know if it was the spirit of the competition or if she was having a great time slinging gingerbread men to customers, but something about her today was even more ravishing. The snug jeans accentuated every perfect curve of hers, and the bright yellow turtleneck sweater clung to her like a second skin. Even the silly gingerbread earrings she wore didn't distract from how stunning she looked today.

I didn't expect to see her in distress when I walked by. She looked miserable and uncomfortable as soon as Kevin stepped closer to her. I don't know what came over me, but one second I was walking back to the tree lot, and the next I was slinging my arm around her waist like I owned her.

And calling myself her boyfriend.

Now, I'm sitting at the Andrews family table for the second time today, waiting for everyone else to show up to get this 'judging' over. I know I'm in last place. I sold seven trees. I let the other volunteers take over most of the sales and tips while I busied myself with wrapping the purchased trees in the netting and helping the customers get them into their wagons. I only chose to carry that extra large tree myself so I could get a peek at everyone else's progress, but I got held up pretending to be a possessive douche of a man.

I stiffen in my chair when I hear the front door open. It's only 5:30, so everyone still has time to get here. I clocked out early to get a quick shower in before stinking up this whole house. I may not have sold many trees, but I did all the heavy lifting. A shower was absolutely necessary before sitting down at this table with Phoebe again.

"Sup Spencey," Piper greets me and sits beside me. "Where's everyone else?"

"Just us so far."

"Oooh, wanna make out?"

I jump back in my seat and look at her incredulously. "What the hell, Piper!"

She cackles loudly and punches my arm. "I'm just kidding you, big oaf! I wouldn't let you near my mouth again with a ten-foot pole." She makes a gagging motion and then settles into seriousness. "For real, though, I can see how much you still want my sister. You can't deny that chemistry between you, even all these years later."

I roll my eyes at her. "Chemistry doesn't mean a thing when our past is still tainted with secrets and lies that I can't share with her." Piper gets quiet and starts tugging at the holes in her jeans. This has always been her nervous tick, and I hate that my stupid comment is the cause of it. "Hey, I'm sorry. I didn't mean it like that," I assure her.

"No, you're right. If I could stop being such a wimp—I'd make both of your lives a heck of a lot easier." She tucks a piece of her dark hair behind her ear and refuses to meet my eyes. "It would make my life easier, to be honest with my family. I'm just not ready to see them look at me with judgment and disappointment in their eyes."

I reach over, place my hand on top of hers, and give it a firm squeeze. Partly because she's about to tear an even bigger hole in her jeans, but mostly because I want to comfort her and feel like a jackass for throwing this in her face in the first place. "I'm sorry, I shouldn't have said anything. You know I'll be here when you are ready. I'll also be here if you never feel ready for that huge step. I'm here, Pipes. Always. We may not have talked over the last few years, but you've always been my best friend. I'm not going to let some stupid crush I have on your sister ruin that. Okay?"

"Besties for the resties, my dude," she jests and smacks my hand away. I'm glad her mood is bright again.

"Please don't ever say that again. I can't cringe any harder than I just did." I shudder mockingly, and we both turn in our seats when we hear the front door open. My hopes drop when I see that it's Austin and Phillip.

"Hey, where's Phoebe at? I thought she was getting a ride with you?" Piper asks her brother before the front door is closed.

"Her and Kevin were right behind us. They should be here any minute." Phil shrugs and takes his place at the table next to Austin.

"What do you mean 'her and Kevin'!" Piper shouts as she slams her hands down on the table and stands up quickly. "Why is he here? Why is she talking to him? Why did you let her stay with him, Phillip?" She stomps out the front door in a rush of fury, leaving us in stunned silence.

"I take it Piper doesn't like this Kevin fellow?" Austin asks.

Phil lets out a loud exhale and folds his hands in front of him on the table. "Let's just say the whole family thinks he's a douchebag.

All of us except for Phoebe, apparently." He shakes his head in frustration. "He invited us all to his home last Christmas after refusing to come here whenever my parents invited him. He claims that he couldn't take time off from work, and because of that, Phoebe also didn't bother trying to come home. It really upset my parents, but they never stopped trying to get her to *want* to be in our lives. We knew she was busy with school and her job at the museum, so we never held that against her," he continues. "So when Kevin invited us up last year, my parents were stoked. They were ready to induct him into the family and make him his personalized stocking to hang here yearly. That is until they met him and saw how much Phoebe had changed around him. It was like this robot took over my sister's body. She wouldn't relax; she hovered around him to make sure he was happy the entire day. It was weird and not like the Phoebe we knew at all. And he just let her! Not once did he make sure she was okay. He just sat back like some rich tool and let her wait on him hand and foot!"

"And that's why they hate Kevin?" I ask quietly. I didn't know about this before seeing him at the market. If I did, I wouldn't have been so polite to him.

"No, they hate Kevin because he left the window open when he asked her to go outside. Right before he dumped her."

I feel a hand pressing down on my shoulder, and I jump out of my seat to see Mr. Andrews hovering behind me.

"That guy broke my Phoebe's heart and didn't have the balls to give her a reason why," Mr. Andrews seethes. "*That* is why we dislike the guy."

Phillip shakes his head in agreement. "Well, Dad, you better get your gun ready because that douchebag is here. With Phoebe."

Mr. Andrews turns redder than Rudolph's nose and squeezes my shoulder tightly before he turns on his heel and stalks out of the front door, slamming it loudly behind him, causing Little E to jump out of the Christmas tree and knock it down before he takes off up the stairs. His gray tail is poofy and wired like a pine needle as it trails behind him.

"Stupid cat," Phillip mutters before standing up to fix the tree. Austin follows him and helps him wrangle all the colorful bulbs and ornaments rolling haphazardly in every direction across the hardwood floor.

We all jump when Piper throws the front door open, pulling Phoebe by her yellow sleeve and dragging her up the stairs. The moment they disappear, Mr. Andrews and Kevin stroll into the house. Mr. Andrews looks less than pleased, and Kevin is shooting daggers my way before he takes in the house's interior.

"Since you all seem to know each other, I won't bother with introductions," Mr. Andrews says gruffly before he looks down at the gold watch on his wrist. "It's 6:00! Whoever wants to have a shot at winning the first task, you have 15 seconds to get your butts to the table!"

I've been a high school football coach for two years, and I don't think I've seen so many people move so fast. Within seconds, we're all seated back at the table, including Kevin, waiting to hear who won this first task. We've handed Mrs. Andrews our sales reports, and she, her husband, and my parents are speaking quietly in the kitchen.

We all wait here in uncomfortable silence, none daring to ask about the fancy coat-wearing elephant in the room. Phoebe has refused to meet my eyes, and Kevin keeps smirking at me like he's in on some secret I don't know about. It's making me itch to punch his perfectly straight teeth out. Phoebe's giving off major 'don't talk to me vibes,' which makes me feel a tad bit better because those vibes also seem to be directed at him. Why is he still here if she's not talking to him?

Our parents return to the room before I've gained the courage to ask her, and we turn our attention to them.

"Alright, kids, the tally is in." Dad gives me a wink before smiling at Phoebe. "Congratulations, Ms. Phoebe, you sold the most items today! Nana gave you a glowing review and said she'd love to have you come volunteer any day of the week. You got her more sales during one shift than she's had all weekend!" He beams at Phoebe, and my heart swells with pride.

"Look at that babe! We won!" Kevin boasts while slamming his hand on the dining table, earning him an entire room of annoyed glances and death glares.

"Don't call me that," Phoebe snaps out. "You dumped me, remember? You don't get to come here and invade my family home and call me that." She stands, grabs her coat and the keys from the small ceramic dish near the front door, and storms out. Running seems to be a family trait.

"Get 'em, girl!" Phillip cheers from across the table, then reaches out to high-five Piper, who has her hand up and ready to go.

Everyone watches Phoebe as she rounds the table and slams the front door behind her. Then, as a collective group, we all death-stare Kevin as he pretends to read something on his phone.

"Alright, kids. Be back tomorrow for task two. 10:00 AM sharp," Dad hollers loudly from the hallway while he helps Mom put on her red winter coat. They live across the street, but the snow has started to pick up, and I worry about them slipping on their short walk over, so I say my goodbyes to everyone at the table, minus Kevin, and follow my parents out.

Once we're outside, Mom stops and places her hand on my arm. "We don't need an escort, dear," Mom says sweetly. "But you could go see if Pheebs is okay. She doesn't seem like herself this evening, and she could probably use a friend." She points at Piper's rental car parked a few houses down and kisses my cheek goodbye.

You know what they say: Mom always knows best.

The Mistletoe Feud 2023
Standings:

Task One: The Christmas Market Salesman
WINNER: PHOEBE

Task Two:
WINNER:

Task Three:
WINNER:

Task Four:
WINNER:

Task Five:
WINNER:

CHAPTER ELEVEN

Phoebe

What is wrong with me?

Am I so broken that I couldn't see what a bad idea this was going to be? Yes, I promised Kevin that I would speak to him. No, that didn't mean I had to let the man drive me to my parents' house.

I'm not an idiot. Well, I'm usually not this big of an idiot. I know how they feel about him. My parents are nothing but loyal when it comes to family, but even more so when it comes to their children.

I chose to let him drive me home. I didn't choose to bring him into the house. I can blame Piper for that, with her combat-ready attitude and innate sense of protection when it comes to me. I planned to let him drop me off, and then we'd make plans for lunch or coffee sometime tomorrow. There was no chance of anyone seeing him if I snuck off after being presented with the next task.

But now, he's here. Sitting in my house. With my family.

And he thinks Spencer and I are a thing, which was funny at first. But now that there's a chance of him saying something about us to my parents, it's not funny anymore.

I need to go back and talk to him and set the record straight. Hearing him call me 'babe' set off every fiber in my body. It felt like my skin would combust in anger, fury, and hatred. Who does he think he is? He can't just come back into my life a year later and act like everything is dandy again.

He doesn't get to ruin Christmas *again*.

I'm all revved up and ready to give Kevin a real piece of my mind when the passenger door opens and Spencer gets in.

"Hey, *babe*. Whatcha doing out here all on your own? Did you forget how to drive while living that subway life in the big city?" Spencer teases, with *my* crooked smile on his lips. The fury spooling in my body mere moments ago has fully evolved into hostile butterflies.

And my goodness, they are flying up a storm right now.

I huff out a defeated laugh. "Funny," is all I say back to him. I don't trust myself not to burst into tears.

"How about we leave all this drama behind and do something fun?"

I glance over, and my eyes meet his. It's the first time all day that I've felt like I don't have to put on this facade of happiness. For whatever reason, I feel more myself around him than I've felt for a long time. I'm not quite ready to dive into what that means, but I know I'm not ready to let it go. Whatever *this* is.

I buckle my seatbelt and put the car in drive. "Where to?"

His answering smile might just light up my entire world.

"Okay, how are you so bad at this!" I cackle while Spencer clings to the guardrail surrounding the ice skating rink. "This was your idea!"

His skates glide unsteadily underneath him as he grips the rail hard enough to make his knuckles turn white. "I never did this as a kid! I assumed you didn't either. Now, watching you skate around me like one of those pros in the flashy dresses on the television, I know that was wishful thinking on my part," he grumbles before his feet slip out from underneath him. Again.

He falls hard on his back, and I have to swallow the laughter trying to claw out of my throat. He's already fallen so many times that I stopped counting, but I admire his persistence. Every time he falls, he gets right back up.

I put my hand out to help him, and he slaps it away and laughs as he stumbles unsteadily back to his feet. "I appreciate the offer, but we'll both end up on our backs if you try to help me." Spencer winks at me and attempts to stretch his back out before he slips and falls to the ice again.

I don't bother trying to hide my giggle when I reach my hand out again, offering to help him to his feet. His hand grips mine, and I feel the chill of his fingertips through my gloves as I struggle to pull him up. His cheeks are flushed red, and I can't tell if it's because of the chill in the air or if he's embarrassed about falling again. I want to think that it's because of me, but I really, really shouldn't let myself go there.

Luckily, there are only a handful of other patrons here tonight, and the other skaters tend to mind their business while gliding on by us. It's sort of a rule of thumb to pretend that everyone knows what they are doing while on the ice and not to make a huge deal about the adults who *will* most definitely fall five hundred times while learning the skill.

"Come on, you'll never learn if you keep leeching yourself onto that rail the entire time." His hand is still grasped in my own, so I tug lightly and help him steady himself without the help of the handrail. He wobbles on his skates for a moment, but he quickly catches his balance. "Here, hold my arm," I tell him, slowly moving his hand to the crook of my arm. "Now, we will go slow until you feel confident enough to let go of my arm."

"Looks like I'll be holding on to you for the rest of my life then," he chuckles and loses his balance again. I use all my strength to keep him upright, and we begin moving around the rink again. "Thanks for this. I know this couldn't have been your idea of a good time when I offered." His expression is too serious as he concentrates on not falling, making it easy for me to keep sneaking peeks at him. I know I shouldn't, but he's so handsome. There is something incredibly sexy about his vulnerability out here on the ice.

"I'm having more fun with you right now than I have over the last couple of days," I confess. "And that makes me feel like a horrible person, but it's also kind of liberating to admit that." I catch his small smile from the corner of my eyes, sending those pesky butterflies free in my stomach again.

"You might feel like a horrible person, but I promise you that feeling the way you feel doesn't make you one. You're allowed to feel overwhelmed and out of sorts, Phoebe. You've been away for a long time, and I can't imagine it's been easy to come back to all this chaos. And by chaos, I mean this whole contest that our parents decided to spring on us," Spencer grins, then continues. "Also, your ex-boyfriend showing up out of the blue can't have been fun for you. Unless you like he's here, that would be alright, too." He gently squeezes my arm but doesn't press me to talk.

"Honestly," I say after a moment of silence passes between us. "I don't know how I feel about Kevin being here. I haven't talked to him in a year and don't want to hear his excuses now. I don't care if he misses me or made the biggest mistake of his life by letting me go," I admit while we carefully glide along the curve of the rink. I love the sound the ice makes when my skateblade goes over it. I catch Spencer's gaze, and he raises an eyebrow at me.

"He waited near the front of the market for me, and as soon as I saw him, I figured I might as well get this talk over with him, so I let him drive me home. He said all the right things. Everything I had been waiting to hear from his lips over the last year. Six months ago, that would have been enough for me to fall right back into being with him," I continue. "But six months ago, I was a mess of a person. A person that didn't know how to love being by herself."

"And you don't feel like that anymore?"

"No, I mean. Maybe? I would be lying if I told you I haven't missed him, he was my closest friend in New York, and when he dumped me I've never felt so alone. But I also don't miss the person I was when I was with him. I'd rather be alone than go back to being that person. I turned into that typical girl who falls head over heels for the handsome, rich mogul of a man. I did everything he wanted. I dressed the way he wanted. I forced myself to like what he liked, even if I hated it. I was walking on eggshells the entire time I was with him, just waiting for him to realize I wasn't the person he wanted me to be."

We get into a steady groove and pick up speed while we talk. I can't believe how easy it is to talk to Spencer. I feel like a teenage girl spilling all my secrets into my diary before bedtime. There's always been something about Spencer. Even as kids, we would talk for hours about everything and nothing at the same time. He was always closer to Piper, but we still had moments of friendship. And I was in love with his teenage self.

"Today just reaffirmed what I've felt for a long time," I say confidently.

"And what's that?" Spencer asks quietly.

"I don't want to be a part of that world anymore. I don't belong in the city. I miss my family. I even miss this tiny town that I couldn't wait to escape. But mostly, I miss myself, the person I was before I got sucked into the corporate life that Kevin lives," I finally admit. To him, to myself. Saying it out loud feels like a boulder has been lifted off my chest. "I don't hate the guy. I just don't want to be the person I was for him any longer."

And I want to quit my job in the city and move home to be closer to my family. I want to meet someone I can make a life with and have silly holiday traditions we can pass down to our kids one day. I don't tell him that last bit, but every part of it is true.

"Anyways," I chuckle, letting out an embarrassed laugh. "Thanks for basically being my unpaid therapist and only friend here," I tell him. "Well, besides Piper, but she's my sister, and she's bound to me because of that whole twin thing. She doesn't get a choice in the matter."

Spencer laughs loudly at that last bit, which makes me smile. I love the sound of his laugh, and I love that even though it's been weird between us, I can still be the one to bring that laugh out of him.

We coast around the rink, making decent speed, and everything feels right in the world again. I know I'll have to go home and talk to Kevin, and at some point, I'll have to break the news to my parents that my fancy art history degree that they helped pay for is basically garbage now. All I want to do is stay in this moment forever, even if Spencer Larson shares it with me.

The lights strung around the ice rink shine brightly against the night sky, and the funnel cake booth gives off the most delicious aromas. The snow is falling softly from the sky, dusting everything in a fresh layer of powder. Everything is perfect.

At least it is until Spencer loses his footing, which brings us both crashing onto the ice. I scream as we fall, and I hear the breath get knocked out of his lungs when I land heavily on top of him. My head is on his chest, and his hands are wrapped protectively around me. We are sprawled out in the middle of the rink. When I lift my head from his chest to look at him, he's already staring at me.

It shouldn't be funny. My elbow is most definitely bruised, and I know he can't feel any better, but suddenly we're laughing hysterically. And it feels good. It feels so damn good to just laugh with him. At him. At us.

I'm still laughing when his eyes meet mine again; this time, his bright hazel eyes aren't filled with laughter and joy. I stop laughing when I realize that the tension between us isn't funny anymore. It's something else. A type of longing shines back at me from his eyes, and I feel my insides melt like butter. The butterflies aren't fluttering anymore. They're nowhere to be found. In their place is a hot, molten feeling, and all I want to do is forget our past and press my lips to his.

He licks his lips, and I feel my body moving involuntarily towards him, which isn't as difficult as one might think while we're sprawled out on the ice like lovesick teens. His breathing picks up underneath my chest. My lungs don't take much convincing to match his. I'm hovering just above him now, looking down at him and his brilliantly sexy eyes that flutter open and close underneath his long lashes as he blinks up at me. The snow falls around us, melting into his sandy blonde hair within seconds of landing. All I want to do is reach up and run my hands through it, to feel the texture of his locks between my gloved fingertips. So I do just that. His eyes close, and his lips part as I softly touch him. I trail my fingers down his face, brow, and nose, then trace his lip softly. He lets out a low moan of pleasure that sends fireworks shooting throughout my entire body. I want to taste that moan with my lips. To taste him everywhere.

I slowly bring my lips to his. A whisper of a kiss sits between us, silently daring the other to make the next move. I feel his breath against my lips, and he opens his eyes to look at me. His brow furrows, his hands grip my shoulders, and he gently pushes me away.

I'm mortified. I mumble out an apology and get to my feet as quickly as I can, my skate slips and I fall on my ass in the process. Spencer gets to his feet and holds his hand out to help me up. I can't even look at him right now, let alone have him touch me again. I refuse his hand and get myself to my feet. My entire body is in a hot flash of embarrassment, and I rush to the rink exit as quickly as my skates can take me. I hear him calling my name behind me, but I can't face him. Not after I just made an epic fool of myself.

I grab my boots from the shoe bin and stumble to the closest bench to rip my skates off, willing myself not to cry. I will not let him see me cry, not again.

He reaches my side when I have both boots on and fully laced up. "Phoebe, I'm sorry," Spencer stammers out. "Please, just let me explain."

"Explain what? That I'm the wrong sister? Again!" I yell out, not bothering to lower my voice when we get nosy glances thrown our way. "I already know that. Trust me, I know. You don't need to remind me. I'm sorry, I'm an idiot and got caught up in the moment. It won't happen again." I stand and head towards the car, leaving him speechless.

When he finally gets into the car ten minutes later, I have nothing to say to him, and he doesn't attempt to talk to me the entire drive home.

CHAPTER TWELVE

Spencer

I don't think I've ever felt this awful before. Well, I guess once before this. When I let Piper kiss me during the Winter formal, even though I invited Phoebe to go as my date. This feeling is worse, though, because she chose me this time. Phoebe wanted me to kiss her back just as badly as I wanted to kiss her. I'll never be able to forgive myself for hurting her again, but I couldn't kiss her, knowing that I've been lying to her for years.

The tension in my gut hasn't gone away, and staring at the streetlights decorated with colorful Christmas lights on my way home doesn't help.

I know I should say something to break the silence stretched taut between us. But I genuinely have no words. I can't believe I let myself blow this one in a million second chance with her. It's no surprise that she's angry at me. She hasn't spoken to me since

I got into the car. Honestly, I'm shocked that she even waited for me. I already had my Uber app up and ready to request a ride when I saw her car still sitting in the small parking lot towards the back of the market. I should apologize to her. I know I've hurt her. But how do I apologize when I can't tell her the real reason why?

She thinks I pulled away because she's not Piper, but that's not it.

I pulled away because I didn't want her to think that there was a universe in which I would choose anyone over her.

I wouldn't.

I couldn't.

Phoebe is seared into my soul, and she's been the only one for me from the first moment I laid eyes on her.

That's what makes all of this so messed up. I can't tell her why I kissed Piper. And because of that, Phoebe will always think she's second best to her sister. I can't make this better without betraying her sister, and I can't betray her sister to get what I desperately want, which is Phoebe.

I'd do anything to go back in time and erase everything between us. To get that real shot at starting over the way it should be. Or, I guess, the way I wish it could be.

Phoebe pulls into her driveway and turns the car off. She hasn't spoken or even looked my way since we left the ice rink, and I can't blame her. If the situation had been reversed and she had pushed me away at that moment, especially after how great of a time we had together, I'd have been upset, too. I may not be able to tell her why, but I can still do my best to apologize.

I run my hands through my hair, working up the courage to speak to her when she exits the car and slams the door hard behind her.

So much for that apology.

I jump out of the car and jog to catch up with her. She's already made it to the house's front steps, and I feel a pang of regret walking up those steps behind her. How was it just yesterday that we were huddled up together on these same steps? Last night, she confided in me and allowed me to comfort her. Tonight, I've gone and made an entire mess of everything again. If I could punch myself in the face, I would.

I reach her and grab her hand before she gets the front door open. "Phoebe, wait. Please just—"

"Just what, Spencer?! Lie to me again about how you don't want Piper. How could I be so stupid? Again!" She yanks her hand out of my grip and crosses her arms. "I don't have time for this, Spence. I really don't. If you want to be with her so badly, be with her. But please," she takes a deep breath before she continues, and I wish I could tell her everything—the whole truth. "Please, just stop toying with me," her voice cracks, and I only want to hold her. But she's right. I can't pursue this until I can give her the entire story, and I can't do that without betraying Piper.

What a mess I've gotten myself into.

The front door opens behind her, and she wipes away the tears that have trailed down her face before turning to see who it is.

Of course, because I can't seem to catch a break for whatever reason, it's Kevin.

"Oh, Kevin," Phoebe gives him a strained smile, then her eyes flash to mine. "What are you still doing here?"

It's not late, but I don't understand why he hung around with Phoebe's family for two hours while we were on our date. Was it a date? Am I even allowed to call it that, considering how horribly it ended?

"I was waiting for you to get back so we could talk," Kevin says while he looks me up and down. I swear his chest puffs out a bit before he turns back to Phoebe. "Can we talk now? Please?"

Phoebe momentarily gnaws on her lower lip, then shakes her head yes to him. "Let's go talk somewhere warm. Hot chocolate sounds delicious right now," she says to him. Kevin's face lights up as he takes her arm and leads her to his car parked on the street. She turns towards me but doesn't meet my gaze. "See you tomorrow for the next task, Spencer."

I stand there with my mouth gaping open and closed like a fish, the apology I owe her caught in my throat as I watch them walk towards Kevin's fancy BMW.

"By the way, Kevin. Spencer and I aren't dating. We were messing around, but nothing was going on between us. Never has been, never will be," Phoebe exclaims loudly.

I'm speechless as Kevin whips his smug-looking face my way. "Thanks for filling me in, *babe*." He opens the car door for her, and I can't do a thing but watch them drive away into the snowy night.

I feel like I single-handedly helped Kevin get another shot at Phoebe. With the way I treated her, I can't even blame her if she falls right back into his arms. I'll have no one to blame but myself.

I planned to wake up early enough to get in a run and then go and pick up some pastries from Adelene's Bakery again. But that plan went down the drain as soon as I opened my eyes and checked my phone and saw that it was already 9:30 AM. I'm supposed to be at the Andrews house by 10:00 AM for the next task.

No, no, no. I can't be late, especially after the way I left things with Phoebe, and the disastrous ending to our "date". I jump out of bed and rush into the bathroom, brushing my teeth and tossing deodorant as quickly as possible. Running into my closet, I toss on the first pieces of clothing that I find: a pair of gray sweatpants and an old Braves sweatshirt that my grandpa gave me years ago.

By 9:45, I'm in my truck and rushing down the highway as safely as possible in the snow, trying to get to the house before they eliminate me from this next task. Even if I'm out of this one, I'll still find a way to get Phoebe the upper hand. I'm glad that Nana didn't tell our parents that I went and bought 100 gingerbread cookies during Phoebe's break and donated them to all the volunteers. I couldn't let Kevin be the reason why she won yesterday's task—even if that makes me feel like a slimeball.

Seventeen minutes later I'm pulling onto the street. I throw my truck in park and rush across the street. Before I reach the driveway, I see Phoebe running up the sidewalk with several large canisters of coffee.

She sees me and stops before picking up the pace again and running up the stairs to the front door. I'm right behind her when she slips, and I catch her under her arms and keep her upright. She scoffs at me, shrugs me off, and runs through the door. I follow her inside and close the door softly behind me.

I'm greeted by Little E wrapping himself between my legs, so I reach down to pick him up and give him some love. He's wearing a bright blue sweater today with little white snowflakes. Maybe if I walk in and everyone sees that Little E still loves me, I won't get eliminated from this round. I'm only 7 minutes late, but I hear everyone "ooooohhhing" Phoebe like we're children and late from recess.

I carry the cat into the dining room, and everyone smirks at me. They know that two of us have just gotten eliminated from this round, giving them a better chance to win today.

I take a seat and look sheepishly around the room. My parents didn't make it over today because Mom had a volunteer shift at the market, but everyone else is here. To my dismay, Kevin is also here. He's helping Phoebe carry in coffee mugs for everyone, and the cocky grin he shoots me when he extends a cup to me makes me see red.

He's just itching to get punched this morning, but I'll behave. I take the mug and tell him thank you with the friendliest smile I can muster on this crap of a morning.

Mr. Andrews comes in a few minutes later wearing yet another sweater that matches Little E's. The room is silent as we drink our hot coffee. "Okay so, y'all know the rules," he nods to Phoebe and I, and she outwardly cringes. "You two were late, so you're eliminated from this task. Sorry, but them's the rules."

Okay, I expected that. It's only fair to hold us accountable, even if I want to throw a fit over the fact that Phoebe was only late because she was bringing everyone coffee.

"Dad," Piper says while looking strangely nervous. Very un-Piper-like, and I'm curious to hear what she says. "Phoebe was only late because I begged her to get coffee since the coffee pot stopped working this morning." She winks at her sister and continues. "And you know I'm all out of sorts with this time change after flying from Germany to be here."

Mr. Andrews narrows his eyes at her and then gives Phoebe the same 'I'm not falling for your bullshit' look.

Phillip adds, "Yeah, and it's not really fair to punish Phoebe for doing us all a solid, right? I mean, she didn't have to bring you coffee, either."

Austin remains quiet next to Phil, but he nods in agreement.

I glance across at Phoebe. Her face is as pale as the snow blanketing the whole town. She's gnawing at her bottom lip again and tugging nervously at her fingers. How can I fix this?

"Also," I chime in with the rest of the group. "Phoebe was only late because I took the last open parking spot on the street. She had to park way down by the stop sign. I watched her jog up the street with both canisters of coffee. It's my fault she was late, and I'll take the blame." Everyone at the table is staring at me now, so I keep going. "I'll sit this task out and the next one. Just don't punish her for trying to do a nice thing for all of us."

Piper raises her coffee mug and yells, "Here, here!"

I look over and risk a glance at Mr. Andrews, and when I meet his eyes, he's smiling at me and silently shaking with laughter. "How about this," he says. "Instead of you missing out on two tasks or missing out on one, why don't you both work together for this next task."

Piper's answering smile is as wide as the Cheshire cats, and Phoebe is much more pale than five minutes ago.

I lock eyes with Phoebe, and we stare at each other with mutual shocked expressions. What have we gotten ourselves into?

"Wait, no fair!" Phil yells. "If they get to partner up, I want to partner with Austin."

"Well, then, I want a partner, too," Piper agrees, crossing her arms and pouting like a child.

Phoebe lets out an irritated groan. "There aren't enough people for all of us to have partners. I'll just sit this one out. It's fine."

"What if I play?"

We all turn and stare at Kevin.

"Umm, no, that's okay," Phoebe laughs at him. "You don't like childish games like this."

"If I get to partner up with you…then I love playing kids' games," he winks at her.

How did I go from trying to help keep Phoebe in the game to assisting Kevin in shooting his shot with her?

Mrs. Andrews walks into the room with a large Santa bowl and steps close to her husband, whispering something in his ear that makes him smile.

"My beautiful wife has just brought a lovely idea to my attention," he kisses her swiftly on the cheek and takes the bowl from her hands. "We decided that we like this idea of partnering you all up, but there's no way you can choose your partners. So my kids will come and pick a name from the bowl. Whichever name you choose will be your partner for the remainder of the tasks."

Now, this is an intriguing turn of events. I don't necessarily love that Kevin is officially joining the game, but I'm hoping that Phoebe doesn't pull his name out of the Santa bowl.

Piper is up first. She grabs a small folded piece of paper out of the bowl and unfolds it quickly. She smiles at Austin and gives him a fist bump from across the table.

Phil shoves his hand into the Santa bowl next, and his groan of frustration has me bouncing on the balls of my feet. Did he get me or Kevin?

"Looks like I'm stuck with Kevin the douche over here," Phil pouts.

Mrs. Andrews claps her hands excitedly. "I guess that means Pheebs and Spencer are partners!" She smiles fondly at her daughter before continuing. "I went ahead and picked the next task for you guys. It's such a perfect day to...build a snow fort!"

We all look at each other, then back at Mrs. Andrews, waiting for her to elaborate because we know that building 'just a snow fort' can't be the task. It's too easy.

"Oh, don't look at me like that! This is going to be fun!" Mrs. Andrews is bouncing in excitement, earning her smiles from us all. You can't be in a bad mood when she's this excited. "Alright, so you girls know how you got me into those blue alien books?" Phoebe and Piper snicker loudly as Mr. Andrews snorts and rolls his eyes at his wife. "Well, I got the idea from them," she continues. "You guys will have to build a snow fort and stock it fully...to last an entire night." She winks in my direction, and I feel my body flush.

Wait, what?

Did she just say that I have to spend the night alone...in a snow fort...with her daughter?

There's a moment of silence at the table, and then Austin, of all people, starts laughing. "You're telling us we have to build a snow fort and spend the night in said snow fort with our partner? That's what you're saying, right?"

Mr. Andrews nods, then looks down at his watch. "You all have until 6:00 PM to have your forts built. I don't care where you build them, but you have to let us judges know by then so we can inspect them. After that, you're on your own until we meet back up at Adalene's Bakery tomorrow at 10:00 AM."

"Get going!" Mrs. Andrews shouts and shoos us all away from the table. "We will see you at 6:00! Make us proud!"

CHAPTER THIRTEEN

Phoebe

This has to be some cosmic freaking joke.

How am I supposed to spend an entire night with Spencer when I can't even look at him without wanting to scream? How are we supposed to work together long enough to build a liveable snow fort?

Why did I turn my mom and Piper onto those stupid alien books? As cute and wholesome and entirely too sexy as they are, I didn't expect them to be the downfall of what feels like my entire life.

I guess I should be happy that I didn't pull Kevin's name. I may or may not have asked him to stay to piss Spencer off. But I don't think I'd be okay with spending an entire night in each other's company after everything we've been through. I probably shouldn't have led the poor guy on, but I was so angry at Spencer for hurting me last night and seeing Kevin at the door after all that—it was surprisingly easy to let him take my mind off it.

Even if all we did was grab hot cocoa from the market and walk around each booth in strained silence. Kevin has this knack for acting like things are fine between us in front of everyone, but when it's just us, he clams up. I don't hate the guy, but nothing is left in that relationship for me anymore. I invited him over for breakfast this morning to tell him just that. Then I got stuck in traffic, and that's how I ended up here.

Partnered up with Spencer while dreading every moment of completing this task with him. I could drop out and tell everyone I don't feel comfortable staying the night in an ice bucket with him. But that wouldn't be true.

When Mom told us that we'd have to stay the night with our partners, I swear my libido went haywire. I'm shocked that no one heard the butterflies take flight in my stomach.

It was stupid of me to get my hopes up with Spencer again last night, but I can't help that my hormones have been kicked into overdrive after our almost kiss on the ice yesterday. I can't ignore that he obviously wants my sister, even if she has had zero interest in him since day one. And I know when she's lying, we share that whole twinster thing, so lying to each other has always been off the table. She doesn't want him like that, and she's pushed me towards him for as long as I can remember. At least, until that kiss between them, which I just unluckily happened to witness,

I want him, and I hate myself for it.

I need to finish packing this stupid overnight bag, and by the time I meet him downstairs, I'll just tell my brain to knock it off. No self-respecting woman would be turned on and excited about being forced to stay the night with a man who is pining after her twin sister.

So, I'll keep repeating my mantra until it becomes engraved into my entire existence, until it becomes barbed wire—wrapped around my pitiful heart.

I will not fall for Spencer Larson.

I cannot fall for Spencer Larson.

Dammit, I shall not fall for Spencer-freaking-Larson.

"So, do you know where we should build our fort?" Spencer asks me as we load his truck up with my things. I didn't pack much, but I have most of the camping essentials. I stole a heavyweight and waterproof sleeping bag from the garage, hand warmers for my pockets, a flashlight, extra socks, multiple changes of clothing that I can layer, and most importantly, everything for smores and hot chocolate. Whatever else we need, we can grab it from the Walmart in town.

"It's been a while since I've camped out, so wherever you think is best is fine with me," I tell him curtly. It's all a part of my plan to talk my brain into not listening to my stupid hormones.

Spencer doesn't respond to that, and instead, we drive in silence for about fifteen minutes along the mountain route. The snow is still falling, but it's not a heavy downfall. It's enough to slowly add inches without completely snowing in everyone around the mountain's base.

After another few minutes of driving, Spencer turns into a narrow street marked only with large boulders. I would have missed this turn entirely if he wasn't here.

"Where are we going?" I ask him, finally breaking the tense silence building between us.

He takes another sharp turn, and we escalate up another narrow gravel road. After about a quarter of a mile, a small cabin appears.

It looks like something out of a movie. Wood log panels line the outside of the cabin, along with a thatched green roof and deep red door. For the holiday season, the door has what looks like a gingerbread man hanging in place of a wreath. There are colorful Christmas lights strung up around the gutters and more wrapped around the small porch. The deck has two dark green Adirondack chairs, with a small table fitted perfectly between them.

He expertly maneuvers the truck into the driveway and parks next to the cabin.

"I figured maybe it would be smart to camp out here for the night, just in case the snow starts really falling," Spencer motions towards the cabin.

"And where are we exactly?"

"My house," he lifts the keys and gives them a playful jingle. "I have everything we might need in the shed out back, and the mountain should block most of the windchill. Nobody said we had to stay in this snow fort the entire time, right?" He flashes a cocky smile towards me, and I find myself smiling back.

"This might be one of the best ideas you've ever had. It's genius!" The excitement in my voice is genuine, and I think maybe this won't be the worst night ever. Worst comes to worst, I'll ditch him and sleep inside the house. My parents didn't leave any actual 'rules' for this task other than build the snow fort and make it liveable for a night. We can make this work.

We exit the truck and he grabs my bag from the back, hoisting it easily over his shoulder before he grabs the sleeping bag and extra supplies I brought. Now that I see what he has in mind, I feel woefully under-prepared. Did I really think one sleeping bag and some hot chocolate would keep me warm all night? I suppose I could have used my lack of expertise to snuggle up with him under the pretense of body heat.

Dear lord, what is wrong with me?

I feel like I'm giving myself whiplash when it comes to my feelings about him. One minute I hate his guts, and the next I can't stop picturing him in bed with me. And yes, rationally, I know that's wrong, but I can't be bothered to care about that right now.

Especially as I watch him carry my bags up the stairs to the cabin door, there is something incredibly sexy about the way those gray sweatpants hug his hips and show off all of his assets.

Nobody said two consenting adults can't have a little fun while stuck in the woods together, right?

"You coming?" Spencer asks from the top of the porch. His voice pulls me out of my inner thoughts like a snap of a whip, and I scurry up the steps behind him as quickly as I can.

He unlocks the front door and kicks it open, motioning me to go in first. I know I was thinking about doing naughty things with him, but being this close to him and stepping into his home—I'm nervous as all get out.

He steps in behind me and places my bags down on the floor. The inside of his house is dark, but the light from the sheer green curtains is enough to see most of the layout. I watch him stroll into the kitchen, open the blinds, and turn on the lights.

"Sorry, it's dark in here. I woke up late and just rushed out," Spencer walks past me again and opens another set of blinds near a small dining table. "Make yourself at home. There's food in the fridge and K-cups for the Keurig. Mugs are in the cabinet next to the fridge."

I mosey my way into the kitchen. It's small but intimately cozy and very, very tidy. There isn't a single dish in the sink, and the granite countertops look perfectly wiped down. He has a tea towel hanging on the stove, and I'm not surprised that it's Christmas-themed.

Seeing all the touches of Christmas throughout the area makes me smile. Kevin didn't even bother putting a tree up, and he wouldn't have bothered to swap out towels or hang a holiday-themed wreath on the door. I practically had to beg him to let me decorate his home for Christmas last year when my family came to visit, and those decorations had to be tactful and elegant to fit the vibe of his home.

Spencer has gingerbread men decor, tiny reindeer, and cute little snowmen decorations placed in random nooks and crannies throughout the kitchen. It's absolutely adorable and makes me curious to see what else he has throughout the house.

I turn on the Keurig and wait for it to warm up. As I wait, I pull two holiday mugs from the cabinet. One is green and shaped like a Christmas tree, and the other is a white snowman. I giggle out loud at the thought of him using these daily.

"What's so funny?"

I jump and turn to find him perched on a barstool I missed when I came in. He's removed his hoodie and has a fitted black v-neck on in lieu of it. Seeing him makes my mouth dry, and instead of answering him, I sheepishly hold up the two mugs.

"Mom got those for me last Christmas at the market. They make excellent hot chocolate mugs."

"Can I use them for coffee?" I ask and look down at both of them, pretending to inspect them thoroughly as an excuse to take my eyes off him.

"I don't see why not," he says in response.

Turning away from him, I quickly make both cups and place the snowman one on the bar in front of him. He grins as he gets up and opens the fridge, then pulls out a bottle of creamer with the Grinch on it. He shakes it, then pours a generous amount into his mug before offering it to me. I take it and snort when I see its flavored 'Snickerdoodle Cookie' before I pour a much smaller amount into my mug.

Spencer opens the drawer behind me, and I stiffen when he softly places his hand on my hip, gently moving me aside so he can grab a spoon. He stirs the creamer into his coffee and sticks the spoon in his mouth. Walking over to the sink, he pulls the spoon from his mouth and starts to place it in the sink. Then he turns back around and sticks that same spoon into *my* cup, stirring it gently and placing it into the sink.

My eyes don't leave him as I watch him sit back on the barstool and sip his coffee. He winks at me when he catches me staring at him, and in a panic, I swallow a large, scalding hot gulp of my own.

Why was that so extremely sexy? I'm practically salivating at the idea of his mouth anywhere near my coffee while also trying not to cough up a lung, as it's on fire thanks to my stupidity.

"Alright, let's do it," Spencer says out of nowhere.

This time, I cough up some of my coffee, but I catch it all in the sleeve of my jacket before looking at him in shock. "Excuse me! Do what?"

He hands me a napkin, and I happily take it from him. Our hand's brush, and that electric shock feeling comes back, forcing me to yank my hand away quickly before I give in and pounce on the man.

"Let's build this snow fort. Have any ideas? Since there aren't 'technically' any rules, we can get away with anything. It just has to be better than everyone else's to win." Spencer blows into his coffee and takes another sip. "And Pheebs," I look up at him and melt a little when I see *my* smile plastered on his face. "We are in it to win it. So let's build the best damn snow fort our parents have ever seen."

He holds his snowman mug out, and I clink my Christmas tree mug to his.

I will not fall for Spencer Larson.

I cannot fall for Spencer Larson.

Dammit, I might be falling for Spencer-freaking-Larson.

CHAPTER FOURTEEN

Spencer

When I woke up this morning, I had no idea my night would end with Phoebe snuggling next to me in front of our small fire, cooking pigs in a blanket, skewer style.

We spent the day as a companionable team, jotting down ideas for this task before running to town for supplies and lunch. We haven't talked about our almost-kiss, and I still owe her a giant apology and explanation. I can do the apology, but the explanation is a bit trickier. I need to talk to Piper soon. But right now, Piper has no place with us in front of our tent.

Yes, I said tent. Since our parents didn't give us any rules for this, we improvised the best we could without having to freeze to death. I fully expected Phoebe to be inside, warm and toasty by the fire. But she's tougher and more stubborn than I remember her being. She's said no countless times to my attempts to get her to go inside and rolled her feisty green eyes even more.

I feel like we cheated, but when our parents came by to judge our poor attempt at a snow fort, they didn't say anything to imply that it was the greatest thing they've ever seen—or the worst.

Our snow fort is constructed with a rectangular two-person tent, a tarp over the top, and stakes around the tent's edges. We took some firewood that I had already cut and made a border around the entire tent, minus the door. After that, we packed as much snow over the tarp as possible, letting the firewood help keep the snow from sliding all the way off.

It looks like a tragic mess just waiting to fall apart the moment we get inside, but it's surprisingly holding up so far. And it was a blast to make with Phoebe. We made so many failed attempts in the process, and most of them ended in laughter and a few snowball fights until we got it right.

Phoebe decided to make a whole shebang out of camping in the wilderness, so while we were at Walmart, she grabbed skewer sticks, hot dogs, and bread dough. Hence, the pigs in a blanket skewer.

I can't stop looking at her. Her red hair looks like brushed copper in the firelight, and her cheeks are flushed red, either from the cold or the heat from the fire. She's got a pair of purple earmuffs on, and she's wearing my Braves sweatshirt, which is huge on her.

Her sweater got soaked during one of our many snowball fights, so I let her borrow that one while hers was in the dryer.

I'd be lying if I said I didn't think her wearing my clothing wasn't a giant turn-on. I don't know how I'm going to sleep next to her all night. I've already had to talk myself down multiple times today...if you know what I mean.

"Pass me that plate," Phoebe motions towards the box of camping supplies I brought out of the shed. "Please," she adds in quickly.

I fish one of the plates out of the box and hand it to her, and she expertly removes the food from both skewers onto the plate.

"When's the last time you camped?" I ask her.

She lays the skewer sticks in the snow and grabs one of the hotdogs from the plate, blowing on it before biting into it. The moan that comes out of her mouth makes me almost drop the plate.

How am I supposed to lay next to this woman all night, knowing she makes noises like that?

She covers her mouth with her hand before she answers. "I haven't camped since high school."

I raise an eyebrow in surprise. "And you just remembered how to make a perfect pig in a blanket years later?"

"Oh, I make these at home all the time. I have one of those metal fire pits on my patio because I cannot survive long without a good s'more." She laughs loudly from behind her hand. "But don't tell anyone. My landlord would throw a fit if he knew I was always making fires out there. There's nothing like curling up by the fire with a good thriller book and a plate of food cooked over the fire."

"I can't say I've tried that, but it sounds nice." I take a bite of my food and look at her in surprise before swallowing. "Phoebe, this is delicious. I promise not to say a word to your landlord if you promise to make me these for the rest of my life."

The smile fades from her face, and she stares into the fire silently as we finish eating. Somehow, I am cursed to always say the wrong things to her. She doesn't say anything as she stands and holds her hand out to me, I reach up slowly, confused and place my hand in hers.

She giggles, breaking the strained silence from moments before. "No dummy, give me your plate. I don't want to leave them out here in case of bears or whatever else wanders around in the night sniffing out food."

Just call me Mr. Dumbass because I sure know how to make an ass out of myself in front of her.

I pull my hand out of hers and hand her my plate. She looks back at me and smiles before she goes through the front door.

Maybe my big mouth hasn't ruined the night after all.

A few minutes later, Phoebe comes out of the house with our two mugs from earlier clutched in her hands. As she gets closer, I see a mound of marshmallows atop both mugs. She hands me the snowman mug and sits next to me on the wooden log I placed in front of the bonfire for us.

"I hope you like hot chocolate," she says, holding her mug out to toast. "I figured this is the perfect night for some since we will be freezing our fingers off here soon." I can't tear my eyes away as she sticks her tongue out and grabs one of the marshmallows, bringing it back to her mouth to eat it. She repeats this several times before I realize I'm staring at her like some sort of creepazoid again.

My marshmallows have melted enough that I can easily take a sip, and when I do, I taste the familiar shock of cinnamon whiskey sliding down my throat. Like the idiot I am, I start coughing up a lung in front of her, and she bursts into laughter.

"I'm sorry! I should have warned you, but I really, really wanted to see your face when you drank it." She snorts into her hand and kicks her feet like a child, which makes me forgive her for the whiskey assault.

"Phoebe Andrews, are you trying to get me drunk?" I raise an eyebrow and give her a sultry look, sipping my hot chocolate again as she catches her breath from laughing so hard.

She takes a deep drink of hers and then turns her body towards me. I'm instantly alert, and my palms start to sweat because I know this is the moment—the moment where she finally asks why I pulled away from her last night. I've been dreading this talk since we got paired up this morning as partners for this task.

I really wish I would have talked to Piper before all this.

She's biting her lower lip again, making her look too vulnerable. "Look," she says as she runs her free hand over her face. "I know this is about to burst this happy little bubble we've pretended to be in all day, but I can't hold this in any longer."

I nod at her, then chug the rest of my drink. The warmth from the whiskey spreads through my chest, calming me slightly. I guess

I'm about to wing this because I can't let her feel like this any longer, but I can't tell her the whole truth.

Half-truths and real feelings will have to do.

She follows suit and downs the rest of her drink, shuddering hard once her cup is empty. "I sort of wish I would have just brought the bottle out because I'm going to need a bit more courage to get all this out." She starts to stand, and I wave my hand to stop her.

"I'll go get it," I tell her and run into the house, grabbing the bottle from the counter where she left it. I take a quick swig of it, relishing in the burn again before returning outside.

When I reach her side again, I hear music, and I can't help but laugh when I recognize the Taylor Swift song coming from her phone.

"What, you don't like her?" Phoebe asks incredulously.

"I didn't say that. I don't mind her music at all. I just didn't expect to hear it, that's all."

Phoebe holds her mug out to me, and I pour her what I think is about a shot into it. She tosses it back right away and holds her mug out again. I raise an eyebrow at her, and before I pour her next shot, I drink a mouthful straight from the bottle. I pour her another shot and screw the cap back on, setting the bottle in the snow between us.

Phoebe takes her ear muffs off, tosses them into the supplies bin, and shakes her hair out. I think my new favorite smell might be campfires and mangoes. I itch to move closer to her and inhale the heady scent. I watch as she tosses her shot back and can't help but love the way she scrunches her face up before swallowing.

"Alright," she says after a full-body shudder. "I need to know why, Spencer."

Here we go.

"Why what, Phoebe?" I know I'm being dense, but I need to hear her say what's on her mind before I spill anything.

She rolls her eyes at me, making me smirk at her. That irritates her even further.

"I just don't understand what I'm missing," Phoebe says in a rush. I furrow my brows in confusion. "Urg, you're going to make me say it. And I'm going to feel even stupider than I feel right now."

"You're not stupid, Phoebe. I want to know what's going on in that mind of yours. I don't want to misinterpret anything."

"Ha. Like I misinterpreted that 'almost kiss' last night." She shrugs and runs her hands through her hair in frustration.

"You didn't, though. Misinterpret that, I mean."

"Then why did you pull away?" My eyes meet hers, and I don't think I've ever seen this expression on her face. The absolute anguish and uncertainty in her eyes. "Am I reading this wrong again? I thought maybe there was something here," she waves her hand between us. "I mean, I don't think it's surprising that I still have feelings for you. Even after all these years, I can't seem to turn them off. And believe me, Spencer, I really wish I could. So, I need to know why I'm not enough for you..." Her voice cracks slightly, and she wipes at her face angrily.

She's left me speechless again. Every fiber in my body screams at me to give in and tell her the truth. Tell her that it's always been her. That there's been no one else but her, and at this rate, I can't ever imagine anyone else taking up space in my heart the way she has. Even as a kid, I knew there was something special about her. Nobody has ever made me feel this alive, this at ease in my own skin.

I should tell her that.

But instead, I say nothing. The silence stretches between us like the last strum of a guitar in the song that just ended on her phone. Long, unyielding, and utterly heartbreaking.

"You're a coward, Spencer," she spits out. Grabbing her phone and the bottle of whiskey at our feet, she storms into the snow fort, leaving me alone to listen to the crackling logs on the fire and regretting every second of my silence.

I put out the fire and then head inside the house to take a quick shower. I change into warm pajamas and grab Phoebe a pair of my warm thermal pants and another sweatshirt that doesn't smell like the campfire before heading back out to the snow fort for the night.

I sit on the porch while trying to give Phoebe space. But it's freezing out here, and it isn't long before I give in and slide the tent's zipper open, squeezing my way into the small space.

Immediately, the air between us is charged. I can't tell if it's due to Phoebe's anger at me or the usual tension that lives and breathes between us at all times.

She's already lying on her side, facing away from the tent's opening. I place the extra pajamas I've brought for her at the foot of my sleeping bag and maneuver myself into the small space dedicated to me.

I pull the blankets over both of us, trying not to disturb her. The space is an extremely tight fit, with the two of us squeezing in together.

Not that I'm complaining. I'm just worried about Phoebe snuggling a little too close because I don't know how to hide that I'm incredibly turned on right now.

So here we are, lying side by side in a two-person tent, sharing multiple layers of covers and huddled together for body warmth.

And she's angry as hell at me.

CHAPTER FIFTEEN

Phoebe

I'm trying to ignore that Spencer's entire body is about an inch away from touching mine. It's not an easy feat, though, when I have to scream at myself to stop slowly inching closer to him to steal some of the body heat coming off of him.

I was angry at him for closing up again and refusing to talk to me. But this was the confirmation I needed to let him go finally—or, I guess, the chance of him.

It's clear now that he enjoys the flirtation between us but wants nothing more than that. It hurts, and I'm incredibly embarrassed. Being forced to be around him right now feels like someone is tugging a rib bone out through my sternum.

Even if the butterflies in my stomach won't stop doing that annoying thing they do anytime he's around me.

His hand touches my thigh, and it feels like fireworks are about to burst out of my skin. I sit up quickly and turn on the flashlight on my phone. My music still plays as I look down at him, not bothering to hide the streaks the tears left on my face.

His hair looks damp, and he's changed into new clothes. I hate that even though he doesn't want me, I want him more than I've ever wanted anything. I haven't been able to escape these feelings toward him. Even running to New York, he was always there, digging his own hole in my soul.

"Phoebe," Spencer whispers as he sits up, making the distance between our mouths only about a foot apart. I watch in fascination as he licks his lips and glances down at my own before making his way back to my eyes. "I'm sorry." I place my finger over his lips, silencing him.

I may never have his heart as I want it, but I don't want to hear his apology right now. I don't need it. I know where we stand, and as much as it hurts, I will have to force my heart to get in line.

But I also don't want to fight any longer and can't keep ignoring this tension between us anymore. If this is my only chance, I don't want to waste it by talking.

And I'm dying to know what he tastes like.

I reach behind me and grab the bottle of whiskey I've been curled up with since I left him at the fire, and I take another long swig of it. I offer it to him, and he takes it with the hand not gripped on my thigh. He places the bottle in his mouth and tips it slowly so I can see his throat working to swallow the cinnamon liquor.

He hands the bottle back to me; my fingers are shaking as I work to screw the cap on tightly before placing it behind me again. □

The edges of the world are fuzzy, and I'm relishing in the warmth that is a constant in my body from the alcohol while also relishing in the desire pooling in his eyes as he gazes at me.

We may not be meant to be each other's happily ever after, but what's stopping us from making this our own version of it?

A version that fits us, and only us.

'Back to December' is playing softly on my phone, and in the words of Ms. Swift, this is me swallowing my pride.

I lean forward and press my lips gently to his.

I wait for him to push me or pull himself away, but that doesn't happen. Instead, he reaches up, cups my face with his hand, and pulls me closer. Kissing me back just as fiercely as I'm kissing him.

Every thought I had before this empties from my head.

There is only this.

Us.

Fireworks explode around us as I open my mouth for him, teasing his tongue with my own. He tastes like cinnamon, and I think that it might just be my new favorite flavor. My hands grip the front of his shirt, pulling him tighter against me as I move to straddle his lap, never breaking contact with his lips. His moan reverberates throughout my entire body when I press myself closer to him, tugging him nearer until there's no space between us except for the barrier of our clothing.

Remember that thing I said about not falling for him?

Well, it's officially too damn late.

His kiss destroys me, leaving a Spencer-shaped hole where my heart used to be.

And I don't care. I'll suffer those consequences later. Right now, all I need is more. More of him, more of this. More of whatever this is between us.

Reaching down, I tug his shirt up, and it's only when I try to pull it over his head that we finally break our kiss. I toss his shirt over my head and run my fingers slowly over his bare chest. I knew he was fit, but I didn't realize he was in this great shape. I wouldn't be surprised to find out he's a secret underwear model as a side job.

Before I go any further, Spencer gently grabs my hands with his own, stopping me and finally forcing me to look at him. His eyes are gleaming with an emotion I don't recognize, but it's more than clear that he's enjoying this as much as I am.

So why is he stopping me?

"Phoebe," his voice sounds deeper than usual, and his breathing ragged. "I just need to say something before this escalates."

I squeeze his hands tight, dread already pooling in my stomach. I told myself I was okay with this only being something physical tonight. But I don't think my ego can handle him confirming that's all he wants, too.

He clears his throat and pulls one of his hands out of my grasp. He gently places it on my cheek, rubbing it back and forth over my overheated skin. He places his forehead against mine. "I've thought about this moment for my entire life, Phoebe. And I don't want to mess it up. I don't want to chase you away again." His breath against mine is a drug I didn't know I needed until this very second, and I never want it to stop. "I've never done this before," he admits shyly.

"Done, what exactly?"

Spencer laughs softly, vibrating our bodies and making me grin like an idiot. I've always loved the sound of his laugh, but being this close and in this position with him, I love it even more. "Okay, you can't laugh at me, or I'll never be able to look at you again. And Pheebs, I really, really love looking at you," he says, and another laugh escapes my lips.

"I promise I won't laugh at you."

He takes a deep breath and releases it slowly between us. "I've never done this," he motions with his hand to the two of us, and I furrow my brow in confusion. "Shit, okay. I'm just going to have to say it, and when I do, I'm going to just melt into a puddle of embarrassment."

"Dude, just spit it out! You're starting to make me nervous."

He closes his eyes and takes another shaky breath. "I'm a virgin."

Oh.

That is not what I was expecting him to say. I was gearing up for the 'I just want to be friends' talk or whatever. But not *this*.

His confession makes the butterflies in my stomach flutter around like crazy. I don't think I've ever been this turned on by words before, and it's taking everything in me not to jump his bones.

Spencer still has his eyes closed tightly, his breathing is heavier, coming out in nervous, ragged pants between us.

Leaning forward again, I press my lips to his cheek, then slowly across his face. Kissing him gently in different spots until he laughs.

"You're taking this better than I expected," he says between my kisses.

I pull back and look at him. "Why wouldn't I? It's like every girl's dream to find a guy she can corrupt with all the scenes from her smut novels. And you, Spencer, are about to be corrupted." I smirk at him and nip at his jaw with my teeth.

His answering groan is like a breath of fresh air, and when our lips meet again, there's a drastic change in the air. Our first kiss seems sweet and innocent compared to this one. I am fueled by fire and lust as he kisses me deeply, fully, passionately.

When we wake up tomorrow, we will be wholly different people, so I'm going to take full advantage of this one night we have together.

It's everything I've ever wanted with him—and everything I can't keep after tonight.

I push him backward onto the sleeping bags and kiss my way down his throat and his chest until I'm kissing and nipping small bites at the edge of his pants. One of his hands is fisted in my hair, and the other is gripping the bedding tightly as his hips thrust slightly at every kiss I place upon his stomach.

I grab the waistline of his pajamas and start to pull them down, a small amount in tandem with every kiss I place in their absence. Before I manage to pull them any further than his hairline, he grabs my wrist, forcing me to stop and look up at him. "What's wrong?"

I ask him, praying that he isn't about to come to his senses, and tell me this is a bad idea. I know it's a bad idea, but I don't care right now.

Bad ideas always start out as fantastic ones if you believe hard enough.

He grabs me under my arms and drags me back up his body until we're kissing again. While I'm confused as to why he stopped me, it's hard to be upset about it while his tongue is meeting mine in perfect rhythm. His teeth bite down on my bottom lip hard enough to make me moan out in pleasure. I run my hands through his hair and fist them tightly as I pull his head back roughly, forcing him to look at me.

"I said, what's wrong?" I give his head a sharp tug again when he tries to come in for another kiss. "I can do this all night, Spence."

The grin on his face is devious and full of mirth. "Nothing is wrong," he says as he kisses the arm lounging on his shoulder. "I just want to pleasure you first."

Oh.

I lean forward and run my tongue up the side of his face, his erection is pressing into my thigh and I can't help myself. I move my thigh up and down, caressing it and making him groan out. The sound makes my libido kick into overdrive, and I want him to touch me. I release his hair and move from his lap, making myself comfortable on our sleeping bags.

"Then have at it," I tell him, spreading my legs as an invitation.

CHAPTER SIXTEEN

Spencer

I don't hesitate to take Phoebe up on her offer. Positioning my body over hers, resting my weight on one of my elbows so as not to crush her, I kiss her thoroughly. Her legs wrap around my waist, and she pulls my hips down to hers. We both still have that barrier of clothing on, but I can feel the body heat blazing off of her, just as I know she can feel my hard-on pressing into her. She doesn't seem to mind it, but if she keeps writhing her body the way she is, I'm not going to last long.

Copying her, I sprinkle kisses down her neck as my hands work on pulling her sweatshirt off. I help her sit up, and she tugs the sweatshirt, along with whatever shirt she was wearing underneath, off. She grabs my face and pulls me back down to her, crushing her lips to mine in frantic movements.

When I break away, she gives me a slight pout, and I reach up and grab her bottom lip. "Don't worry, baby, I'll make use of these later," I promise her and kiss her hard, making her gasp and moan against my lips.

I almost burst at the seams, but I need to give her what her body desperately demands.

I return to my assault of kisses, starting at her neck and trailing my lips and tongue down to her breasts. I tug her bra down, and the snarl of pleasure that escapes my lips is feral as I look at her breasts. Perfection. She is utterly perfect in every way. Circling my tongue around her peaked nipple makes her scream out, silencing the music that's filled the small tent. I work on one nipple with my mouth and use my fingers to pull gently on the other. Her back bows off the bedding, and she thrusts her hands into my hair, pushing my face harder into her breast.

Whatever she wants tonight, she gets.

I move my mouth to her other nipple and bite down gently as my fingers circle the one I just left.

"Oh god, Spencer! Yes! Just like that!" Her legs tighten around me again as she yells out, grabbing my hair harder.

But I don't want her to finish yet. I want to taste her orgasm. I make my way down, leaving trails of kisses down her stomach, and when I reach her waistband, she lifts her hips so I can take her pants off. I rub my hands over her bare legs and notice the goosebumps that have covered them.

"Let's get you under the covers, baby. I like my dessert nice and warm." I wink at her when her jaw drops.

"Spencer!" She swats at me playfully before she situates herself under the heap of blankets.

I join her under the covers, picking up where I left off. I slowly inch her lace panties down her body, kissing and teasing her gorgeously long legs with my mouth as I go. She helps push them off, and I make my way back up, kissing her inner thighs and making her groan in response.

I pause, and my mouth hovers right above her entrance. Suddenly, I'm second-guessing myself. I've never done this before and don't want to disappoint her.

She runs a hand through my hair, and when I look up at her, she smiles at me, then runs her hand down my cheek. "Just do whatever feels natural to you. If you don't like it, we stop. Yeah?"

God, it would be so easy to love this woman.

I nod at her in understanding, and then I turn my attention back to what I was doing before I started to chicken out. I run my fingers over her, searching for the spot that makes her tick. When I find it, she bucks her hips off the ground and moans words of encouragement while fisting her hands into my hair and pulling me further to her. I replace my fingers with my tongue. Licking her thoroughly and deeply while my fingers enter her and tease her from the inside until she's screaming out my name and convulsing around me.

I could die from this. Listening to her pants and moans. I wish I could bottle up her taste and hear her scream my name repeatedly for the rest of our lives.

"Oh my god," she huffs out. Her breath comes in quick pants as she tries to catch her breath.

I can't tell if I'm more turned on by her screaming my name the way she did or by the fact that I brought this glow of pleasure to her. Either way, I'm basking in the heady aftermath of what I just did.

"Spencer, that was amazing. Perfect even. I've never come that fast before," she giggles, and the sound is music to my ears. "You'll have to give me a moment. I'm pretty sure my legs are made of jello right now. I can't believe I let you give me an orgasm while Taylor Swift was playing!" She laughs loudly and covers her face with her hands.

I move until I'm lying next to her, our faces mere inches from each other as I stroke her body softly with my fingers. "Keep covering this beautiful face of yours up, and I'll make you come twice." I pull her hands away from her and flash her my best cocky smile. Which I hope looks just as cocky as I feel right now.

Phoebe flicks my nose, causing me to laugh loudly this time. "I wouldn't be opposed to that, but if you give me another orgasm like that, I won't be able to keep my eyes open any longer." She yawns loudly.

"Do you want to call it a night? We have to get up early tomorrow to meet everyone for breakfast."

"Absolutely not," Phoebe says, sitting up quickly. "It's my turn now." Her smile lights up the entire tent before she sneaks under the covers and takes me in her hand. Then, her mouth. The feeling is absolutely mind-blowing, and I let her take charge while my eyes roll to the back of my head.

I didn't last long after that, much to my embarrassment. But I wouldn't change a damn thing about this night. I've waited my whole life to share this moment with her, and it was even better than all of the fantasies I've conjured up in my head over the years.

We spend the rest of the night wrapped in each other's arms.

I wish I could end every night like this, with her breathing softly against me, her red hair sprawled over my pillow, and her body pressed tightly against mine.

Sadly, I know that the morning will bring us back to reality, and my reality still includes secrets and lies that I can't share with her. This might be our first and last night spent like this together. I pull her closer and kiss her forehead, whispering words of gratitude to whatever higher power is up there for letting us have this small slice of happiness, even if it'll all be gone when the sun rises.

I'm jarred awake as Phoebe pushes her way out of the blankets. She unzips the opening of the tent quickly and rushes through it. I grab her boots and an extra blanket before running through the opening after her. The morning sun is blinding against my eyes as I try to find which direction she went. Raising my hand to block the bright rays, I see her hurling her guts out at the edge of the stairs leading up to the front door.

Quickly making my way over to her, I throw the blanket around her shoulders and drop her boots into the snow behind us. I rub circles on her back while she heaves repeatedly. She tries pushing me away, but her attempts are feeble, and I refuse to leave her alone out here while she's sick like this.

When a minute or two go by, and she doesn't puke again, I grab her from under her knees and cradle her to my chest, carrying her up the steps to the front door. I never locked it last night, and while I'd usually berate myself for being so careless, I'm okay with it for now because it makes carrying her into the house that much easier. I open the door and gently set her on the couch, pulling the yellow throw blanket from the back of the sofa and tucking it into her as best as possible.

I put my hand on her forehead but can't gauge her temperature because we just spent the night in the Arctic. "What can I do? What do you need?" I ask her while frantically running my hands over her body, like I can somehow sense what's wrong with her with just my touch.

She tries to sit up, grabbing my hand for support until she's sitting against the back of the couch with her head thrown back. She squeezes my hand tightly, and in the same second, her face turns an unnatural shade of green. I jump up, grab the trashcan from under the kitchen sink, and make it back to her just as she starts to vomit again. I'm unsure how to help, so I move behind the couch and hold her hair out of her face until her puking episode subsides again.

Phoebe throws her head back on the headrest, runs a shaky hand down her face, and then looks up at me. She gives me a weak smile. "I'm so freaking hungover," she mumbles out.

Well, that makes sense. She had half a bottle of Fireball to herself last night, and she's not a large person. Mix a small amount of food and no water between shots—it's basically a hangover cocktail.

I run my hands over her forehead to make sure she's not feverish, and she grabs my hand and presses it against her cheek. "Your hands are so cold," she groans out. I try to pull my hand away, thinking the temperature is bothering her, but she holds it firmly. "No stay, please. It feels amazing."

Her alarm goes off minutes later, and she fishes it out of the sweatshirt she borrowed from me last night. "Oh, crap! We need to get to the bakery!" She jumps off the couch and sways back and forth where she stands.

"Oh no, you can stay here and nurse your hangover. I'll go to Adalene's and get our next task," I tell her firmly. There is no way I'm making her deal with all this feud nonsense when she feels this poorly.

Phoebe sits back down, cradling her head over the trashcan I placed at her feet. "What if we get eliminated? Dad said if we didn't show up, we wouldn't join in on the next task."

I walk into the kitchen, grab her a cold Sprite from the fridge, Saltine crackers, and marshmallows, and bring them over to her. I place it all on the coffee table and grab the remote from the armchair I usually occupy during my days off. "You stay here. Rules are meant to be broken. After all, when have we ever been allowed to partner up in this game?" I flash her a smile and place a quick kiss on her forehead before making my way into my bedroom and changing.

When I return, she's lying comfortably on my couch and watching *Game of Thrones*, taking small sips of the Sprite I left for her. I grab my keys and kiss her cheek goodbye before heading out.

I really could get used to this.

CHAPTER SEVENTEEN

Phoebe

Aside from the massive hangover that I 100% inflicted on myself, last night was...wow. I don't think there are enough words in the English language to describe how truly wonderful last night was. I've never been able to get off from oral before, and it's hard to believe that it was Spencer's first time, too. Because he was really freaking great at it. I saw a side of him that nobody else in the world has seen, at least I hope not. He said he was a virgin, but I guess that doesn't mean he's never fooled around with anyone before.

The thought leaves a sour taste in my mouth that fits right in with the taste of my own vomit. However, I'm pretty sure last night was his first time. The look of hesitation in his eyes before he went down on me—there's no way he's done that before with anyone else. *That* thought leaves me giddy with those pesky butterflies.

My phone buzzes loudly from its spot on the coffee table, and when I grab it, I see that it's an incoming Facetime call from Piper. I feel like death, but I'm curious if Spencer made it to the bakery in time, so I hit answer.

Piper's face shows up right as she's shoveling a large maple bar into her mouth. "Oh my—you answered!" she yells, not caring one bit that her mouth is full of donuts. "You look like death, dude."

"Urg. I feel even worse," I tell her. "Did Spencer make it in time?"

"Yeah, he's here. He's talking to Dad right now. Hold on."

"No, you don't need—" I stop mid-sentence when Piper and Spencer show up together on the small screen. Every thought leaves my body when I see them together, pressed so closely and effortlessly together.

Envy.

That's the feeling flooding my bones right now. I know Piper has zero interest in Spencer, but seeing them together so soon after what we did last night. Jealousy overcomes me.

"You feeling any better, Pheebs?" Spencer asks. He pulls the phone out of Piper's hands and walks somewhere more private. It looks like it might be the hallway to the bathrooms at Adalene's Bakery. "Hey, what's wrong?"

Tears well up behind my eyes, and I feel so damn stupid. So stupid for allowing myself to forget that he's always wanted my sister. Stupid for letting him replace her body with mine last night. Was he thinking about her the entire time?

"Phoebe, talk to me," Spencer says, his voice full of concern. "Please?"

I put the phone down for a second to calm myself. I will not let him see me cry. When I lift it back up, he's still there with that same look of concern in his eyes, waiting patiently for me to answer.

"I'm fine, just tired. I'm going to take a shower. I'll see you when you get back," I tell him quickly, trying to keep my voice steady so he doesn't hear it about to crack with unshed tears. "Bye, Spencer. Drive safe."

I hang up on him before he can get another word in, and I finally let the tears I've been holding back flood out. I'm the biggest idiot in the world to think I could do this. To have him for one night and be okay with the aftermath. Seeing him with Piper, though, well, that really hurt. It just brings back all the feelings of doubt and inadequacy I've felt my entire life. He's always wanted her, and I'm a fool for letting myself forget that.

After a much-needed hot shower, I'm feeling a little better. I've put on my favorite Dalmatian print pajama pants and stolen another one of Spencer's oversized sweatshirts because I just really enjoy torturing myself.

I had planned on going out to our poor attempt at a snow fort to clean up while he was gone, but the second I opened the door and got blasted with the frigid air, I decided I'd wait on him to help with all that. I'm not sure I can stomach going into the tent right now.

My stomach is still on the topsy-turvy side, so I'm nibbling on the crackers Spencer left for me. I'm rewatching *Game of Thrones* and trying to quiet the incessant voice in my head that keeps reminding me that Spencer doesn't want *me*. I'm just a copy-and-paste backup version of Piper, and I hate myself for feeling this way. I'm not mad at her, but I'm jealous of her for something she can't control.

That might be worse.

The front door to the cabin opens slowly, and I hear my mother's voice. "Phoebe, hunny, are you in here?"

"Mom! What are you doing here?"

The sight of my mom makes me want to cry all over again. She walks over to the living room, sits beside me on the couch, and pulls me into a warm hug. She smells like freshly baked cookies and home.

She rubs circles on my back, much like she used to do when I was a kid, and overwhelmed with all sorts of emotions that were just too big for me to carry alone.

Not much has changed, huh?

"Spencer said you weren't feeling well, so I brought you some soup and figured I'd keep you company until he returned."

I hug her tighter before pulling away to get a good look at her. My mom has always been my favorite person in the world, with her kind eyes, warm smile, and giant heart. Her red hair is a shade or so darker than mine, though now it's streaked with fashionable grays and pinned up on the side with a shiny snowflake clasp. Every day during the holidays, she wears a different Christmas sweater. Today, she is wearing a bright yellow one with Snoopy in a Santa hat beside his tiny tree. The sight alone makes me want to smile and cry at the same time. I'm an emotional casserole today, and I need to get it together before I spill any beans about what happened between Spencer and me last night. My mom has a knack for pulling out all the nitty gritty details of our life.

"Thanks for the soup, Mama. I appreciate it." I pick up the big container of soup she left on the coffee table and walk over to the kitchen as she follows me.

She opens multiple cabinets until she finds two baby blue bowls and scoops a large helping of chicken noodle soup for each of us. My mouth is already watering. Mom's chicken noodle soup is the absolute best cure for any type of illness, including self-induced cinnamon-smelling ones.

We eat our soup in silence—well, mostly silence. It's the Red Wedding episode, so there's just a tad bit of death and carnage going on as background noise.

"I can't believe you still like this show." Mom chuckles and shudders. "I can't handle all the gore. It's too depressing, especially when they make you fall in love with a character just to let him get his head chopped off a few episodes later! Or worse, stabbed to death in front of their mother!" She shakes her head in indignation. "It's too sad, Pheebs! Too darn sad!"

I chuckle into my soup. My mom has always teased me over my dark choices in television shows. "So, what's the next task? Wait, did we get eliminated because I wasn't there?!"

"Well, your father wanted to eliminate you. You know how he lives for the drama," she tells me, fondness clear in her voice. "Spencer though...he was very adamant about keeping you two in the game. He argued with your dad for about twenty minutes until he gave in. He's a keeper, that one."

"Ha. Yeah, sure he is," I mumble under my breath, taking another bite of soup to wash down the lingering hurt feelings I have about Spencer and Piper hanging out together on Facetime earlier.

Mom surprises me by reaching across the small island and grabbing my hand. "Honey, you know that boy has been in love with you for years. Why haven't you given him a chance?" Her voice is kind and so full of love. "Is it because of Kevin?"

A long sigh escapes my lips as I stare down at my reflection in the leftover broth. I don't want to talk about Spencer or Kevin, but I also really need to talk about it. I've never been good at being alone in my own head, letting my thoughts haunt me on repeat until I'm left a blubbering mess. "Kevin and I...we are done. I was going to tell him to go home yesterday morning before everything happened," I tell her, unable to meet her eyes. "He knows that our relationship is over. What we had was fun, but it wasn't a forever kind of thing. Even if, at one point, I hoped that it was. He's a good man, but he's not—"

Mom cuts me off. "He's not Spencer."

This time, I look up and meet her gaze. Her eyes are kind as always, and there is so much understanding in them reflecting at me. I force myself to take a deep breath, fighting back the tears that prickle behind my eyes. "Spencer likes Piper, Mom. He's always liked her," I admit, chewing on my bottom lip to keep the tears at bay.

Mom stands up angrily and comes to my side of the kitchen island. She grabs my face in her warm hands and forces me to look at her. "Phoebe Lynn Andrews, how can you be so blind?" I roll my eyes at her, and she glares at me like she used to if any of us had rolled our eyes at her when we were younger. "Roll those eyes of yours all you want, young lady," she chastises me. "But you will listen, and you will listen well." I sit up straighter on my stool. "That boy has only had eyes for you. You and only you. I don't know what makes you think he likes your sister, but I'm telling you, you're wrong. I've never seen Spencer light up the way he lights up around you. You. Not Piper. YOU."

"You don't know the whole story, Mom," I counter. "There's a whole past that nobody else knows about."

"Maybe *you* don't know the whole story. Maybe you should ask him and ask Piper. Because I'm telling you, that boy would lasso the moon for you if you let him." She pulls me in and kisses both cheeks, wiping the stray tear away that's making its traitorous way down my face.

We both break apart when we hear the front door open. I quickly wipe my face and turn around to face Spencer.

Urg, he's gorgeous.

His smile is bright and cheerful as he comes in and wraps Mom into a hug. His eyes meet mine over her shoulder, and I feel the blush creeping over my cheeks. I tear my eyes away from him and grab the two empty soup bowls, carrying them to the sink to wash them while they make small talk.

Mom comes over and kisses my cheek, telling me goodbye, and I watch from the sink as Spencer walks her out. My heart rate kicks into overdrive the minute the door closes behind them. How am I supposed to spend a whole day with him again? I can't even look at him without thinking of his lips on mine, on my body...

I jump when he opens the door loudly, letting it bang against the wall. He has his hands full with groceries in brown paper bags. I dry my hands quickly on the festive tea towel and rush over to help him.

"There's more groceries in the back of the truck. Do you mind grabbing those?"

I nod and head outside to fetch them.

When all the groceries are inside, he removes everything from each bag and places it on the round dining table. There are about ten cans of different-colored frosting, multiple bags containing various types of candy, and two large gingerbread house kits.

"Are we making a gingerbread house?" I ask him as I pick up one of the kits and inspect it.

"Yes, ma'am. Your dad's idea," Spencer answers back. He hums in excitement, and I feel my nerves easing up. We won't have to discuss anything if we focus on this next task.

"The next task is a gingerbread house? Seems sort of easy compared to the last two."

He laughs loudly. "We have to build a gingerbread house, but it can't be a gingerbread house."

I raise an eyebrow at him. "What does that even mean?"

"The next task is to build something out of gingerbread, but it can't be a house. It can be a spaceship or the Iron Throne," he motions to the television, which still plays *Game of Thrones*. "It can be whatever wild thing we can think of—"

I cut him off with a laugh. "Except a house. Good one, Dad."

"Bacon and Phil won the snow-fort contest, so we need to really knock this one out of the park."

"Bacon?"

His cheeks flush red, and he runs a hand through his messy hair. "Uh, yeah. Sorry. I meant Kevin." He looks at me sheepishly.

And I burst into uncontrollable laughter.

The Mistletoe Feud 2023 Standings:

Task One: The Christmas Market Salesman
WINNER: PHOEBE

Task Two: Surviving the Snow-Fort
WINNER: PHIL & KEVIN

Task Three:
WINNER:

Task Four:
WINNER:

Task Five:
WINNER:

CHAPTER EIGHTEEN

Spencer

Phoebe's laughter is contagious. I find myself unable to stop smiling because of it, unable to look away from her. I was worried something was off with her when Piper Facetimed her earlier, but with how hard she's laughing, I'm guessing everything is okay again.

Maybe I was overthinking it earlier, and she seemed out of sorts because she wasn't feeling well. Things seem back to normal, though—as normal as they could be considering everything that happened between us last night.

I hope she doesn't regret it. I sure as hell don't. Last night was one of the best nights of my life, and I'm dying to press my lips to hers again. I don't want to spook her, though, so I'll wait for her to make the next move.

The last thing I want to do is drive her away again. Not when things seem to be going surprisingly well between us right now.

Phoebe wipes at the tears streaming down her face from laughing so hard. I don't think I've seen her look more beautiful. Her red hair is in a messy bun piled on her head. She's got on the most ridiculous-looking pajama pants I've ever seen, and she has one of my football sweatshirts. Add all that in with her smile that lights up my whole world. She's perfect.

"Okay, okay," Phoebe proclaims. "I'm done laughing." I raise an eyebrow at her, which sends her into another fit of giggles.

I shake my head at her, laughing at her in the process, and start opening the first gingerbread house kit. I tear the box apart and lay it flat on the table so we can use the cardboard as a base for the project. I'm completely winging this thing, and I hope to make it look like I'm picturing it in my head.

My plan is to build a gingerbread library. We can use some Red Vines and frosting to make bookshelves that line the inner walls of the library, and different types of candy for the books. The rest...well, I'll leave that up to Phoebe because she's got fantastic decorating skills. Her ugly sweaters have won first place every time we've played the Feud over the years, and I know most of them she's made herself.

"Alright, I'm actually done this time," Phoebe giggles while wiping under her eyes again. "Tell me what the plan is. I see those gears working in your head, so fill me in." She steps closer to me, placing her hands on her hips. Evidently, that's her battle stance.

"We need to win this one. We can't let Phil and Bacon get another win under their belts. Sorry, *Kevin*. I was thinking we could make a gingerbread library. We could use different candies as books and line the walls with licorice or something to make it look like bookshelves," I tell her. "Maybe we can use some graham crackers and pretzels to make the tables for our gingerbread men and women to study at. I don't know. I'm just spit-balling here. What do you think?"

She studies the table and the supplies for a moment. "We could get some of those little chocolate donuts and use them as bean bags. I loved the bean bags at my library," she says thoughtfully. "And maybe some of those pink Snoballs can be used as cute little bushes for the front? We can use some green sprinkles to make them look more like bushes, and then we can use red M&M's to make them look like rose bushes. Oh! We can also get some marshmallows and pretzel sticks to make bookcases between the tables, like a real library!" She claps excitedly and jumps up in place.

I glance down at my watch. "We only have a few hours to finish this, so I'll run to the store and grab the rest of the supplies. You stay here and start putting this library together. If that's okay with you?"

Phoebe doesn't say anything, but she quickly walks to the fridge, grabs my grocery list off of it, and then grabs a pen from the junk drawer. I know I need to focus on this task, but I sort of love that she knows her way around my house.

She writes the list in a rush and hands it to me. "Don't forget the peppermint candies! They'll make cute wall decorations!" I love hearing the excitement in her voice. She follows me to the door, and walks me out. She surprises me by placing a swift kiss on my cheek before she heads back inside.

"Oh, and Spencer," she yells from the doorway. I turn back around and face her. "Drive safe."

Her smile could melt all the ice caps in the world with how brightly it shines at me.

When I get home, I don't even reach the front door before I hear Phoebe singing loudly to the *Game of Thrones* theme song. I'm not sure I can classify it as singing since the theme song has no words—but whatever it is—it's loud. I open the door cautiously and almost die of laughter when I see her dancing around in those stupid pajama pants around the kitchen island. She's moved everything I had set up on the table over to the island, and when I step closer to her, I swear I hear her saying something that sounds eerily similar to "wiener" repeatedly in tune with the theme song.

"Phoebe!" I shout over the music. She yells out and jumps, turning around in a flash to face me. She has frosting smeared across her cheek and a piece of licorice hanging out of her mouth. "Are you singing 'wiener'?"

Her face flushes bright red, matching her licorice perfectly. She grabs the remote from the counter and lowers the volume on the television. "Umm, yes?"

"May I ask why?" I set the grocery bags on the counter and cross my arms over my chest. A smile tugs on my lips as I try not to laugh at how adorable she looks.

She yanks the candy out of her mouth and blows out a frustrated breath. "Because I'm a child, Spencer. And because Piper and I watched that stupid *Game of Thrones* parody episode that *South Park* did, and now anytime I hear this stupid song, I have "wieners" on repeat in my head."

"I see." I cover my mouth with my hand, trying to stifle the laughter moments away from exploding out of me.

She rolls her eyes at me. "Just get it out of your system so we can work on this library." She grabs the remote and rewinds it to the start of the opening song, then uses the remote as a microphone while screaming wieners over and over again.

I lose it and almost piss my pants from laughing so hard, which makes her laugh even louder than I am as I run to the bathroom to relieve myself.

When I come out, she's back to working on the library. She hands me a pack of licorice and tells me to start on the other wall. I watch her as she puts together her side and copy her as best as I can. Her shelves are much straighter than mine, but once the candy books are added in, I don't think anyone will be able to notice.

Her expression is serious as she continues to work. Her fingers are nimble and sure with each tiny detail she adds. Phoebe's attention to detail is impeccable, and it makes sense why she chose to work in the art field. The museum she works at must love her. She's not easily swayed from a task at hand. Whenever I try to distract her, she rolls her eyes in response and gives me my next task. We work on separate sides of the library, and after a couple of hours we've made some serious progress. The only thing left to do is add the roof and some more finishing touches on the inside.

The walls are lined with candy bookshelves and filled with candy books. The donut bean bags are grouped in the middle, with a small table made out of chocolate chip cookies, marshmallows, and pretzel sticks in the center of them. Phoebe has even made a small vase using a green Mike and Ike, a red gumdrop, and a toothpick through the middle of them to keep it in place on the small table. We've made the librarian's desk out of graham crackers, and Phoebe has used different types of Hershey's bars to make it look like a pile of stacked books on top of it. The bookcases in the middle have gingerbread men in between them, making it look like they are perusing the books.

We both stand on our respective sides of the island, admiring our work.

"If this doesn't win, then we might just have to take out the judges," Phoebe jokes. "This is amazing, Spence. How did we turn all this candy into this—this freaking masterpiece!"

"I guess we just make a good team," I tease, slowly making my way to her side.

She turns towards me as I place my hands on her hips. "I guess we do," she whispers. "Who would have thought? After all this time, we'd work so well together."

I run my nose against her cheek, inhaling the tantalizing scent of hers. She whimpers softly into my ear, and I glance at the clock on the stove behind her. We have an hour before we need to pack up our gingerbread library and get to her house for the judging.

She'll be returning to the city before New Year's, so I plan to take advantage of our time together. I grab her around her thighs and lift her onto the counter, wrapping her legs around my body as I do. Her hands sneak around my neck, and she grips the back of my hair tighter when I start to tease her earlobe with my tongue.

"You smell delectable as always," I groan into her hair. Mangoes, with a mix of my own body wash that I'm assuming she used this morning during her shower. The thought of her naked in my shower makes me ravenous for her. To taste her again. To have her screaming out my name as she shudders around me once more.

She yanks back on my hair, forcing me face to face with her. "You are very distracting, Mr. Larson. We're supposed to be getting this task done, but you have other plans for us, don't you?" She mewls before leaning in and kissing me soundly, thoroughly.

I could get lost in her kisses. The way her lips seem to fit mine perfectly and the way her tongue wrestles mine for dominance over and over again. Last night, we were both intoxicated on cinnamon whiskey, but right now, I'm just intoxicated on her.

I can't get enough. I need more of her.

Grasping her thighs again, I pull her to me and carry her into my bedroom, placing her gently on the bed without breaking our kiss. She moans into my mouth, making me even harder than I thought I could get. Slipping my hand up her shirt, I am pleased she's not wearing a bra under my sweatshirt. I tease her nipples until they are taut and hard under my fingers. Each playful tug gifts me another of her heady moans until she begs for more. I bring my hand to the waistband of her ridiculous pajamas and then slip my hand further and further until I'm met with the dampness of her arousal.

"Are you needy for me again, baby?" My voice softly caresses her ear.

"God, yes. Please." She bucks her hips into my hand as I slip a single finger into her. In and out, nice and slowly.

"Do you want me to make you come with my fingers this time? Or shall I use my tongue again?" Her breathing is becoming more erratic with my slow and steady assault.

"Fingers," she moans, biting her bottom lip and gripping my bed sheets tightly in her fist.

"My pleasure, Phoebe." I continue until she's writhing underneath me. She groans loudly when I add a second finger into the mix, clutching the bedding as she grinds against my hand. I bring my thumb and rub it over her core until she's screaming as she climaxes around my fingers.

Her body relaxes, and I remove my hand from her pants. Her eyes are wide as she watches me bring my fingers to my mouth and sucking them clean. "Mangoes might be my new favorite fruit, baby."

"You did not just do that! Or say that!" Phoebe hides her face in embarrassment, and I can't help but laugh at her reaction. "It's tough for me to believe that you were a virgin before all this," she says between her hands. "There's no way you should be this good at—"

"Making you come?" I smirk at her as she peeks through her fingers.

"Well, yes. But also have some tact! I can't handle all the dirty things spewing out of your mouth!" She sits up and pulls me by the hem of my shirt, bringing me down to her level, balancing on my elbows above her again.

I kiss her nose softly. "I promise there's been no one else but you, Phoebe." I kiss her cheeks. "No one."

She runs her hands down my chest, stopping at the hem of my pants. "Well, I guess I should return the favor." Her voice is sultry and full of promise as she reaches in and rubs her palm over me.

I hiss through my teeth at the feeling. "I don't want you to feel like you have to reciprocate," I groan out as she wraps her fingers around me, pumping me nice and slow.

"Shhh..." Phoebe whispers while placing swift, chaste kisses on my lips. "Trust me, I want to. I want to make you feel as good as you've made me. I want to feel you pumping through your orgasm, just like you felt mine."

This woman is going to be the death of me. And I'm going to enjoy every torturous moment of it.

CHAPTER NINETEEN

Phoebe

I t wasn't easy getting our gingerbread library from Spencer's house all the way to my parents' house. After a few very careful maneuvers and several close calls that would have ended in devastation, we made it with over twenty minutes to spare. Spencer decided to pay his parents a quick visit while we waited for the others to show up. So, I'm helping my mom whip up dinner for everyone and anxiously waiting for him to return.

I know the excited, giddy feelings I have in my stomach are a terrible idea. Yes, we've had a couple of pretty great hook-up sessions. And yes, Spencer has said some pretty wonderful things about me...

But that nagging voice that keeps screaming that I'm just a backup version of Piper to him won't shut up. I know it's wrong to keep pursuing this, but when he looks at me with that sexy, intense look in his eyes—I'm putty in his hands. Every time he kisses me, my heart and brain play tug-of-war, and it seems like my heart wins every time. I can't stop myself from making bad choices when it comes to him.

I need to talk to Piper about what happened all those years ago. I need verbal confirmation from her that it's okay for me to pursue him. Even though I've sort of already crossed multiple lines with him, I won't go any further with him until I know she does not—and will never—want him.

I need to talk to Spencer, too. I have to know if he still feels anything for my sister. And I need to know why he kissed her if he was supposedly waiting his entire life for me.

I can't seem to wrap my head around it all.

Until I have the guts to voice these concerns with him and Piper, I'll be elbow-deep into mashing these potatoes for this sweet potato casserole I'm helping Mom make.

"What's going on in that head of yours, darling?" Dad asks me as he sneaks a bite of ham Mom is carving. I lean into him when he comes over and kisses my cheek. I may be in my twenties, but I'll never get tired of these little moments of affection from him.

I turn my focus back to spreading the potato mash into the glass bakeware that Mom laid out for me. "Not much, just ready to be crowned the Mistletoe Queen," I say with an obvious smugness, earning a loud chuckle from Dad. "Did you check out our gingerbread library?" I ask him while I put the casserole in the broiler and set the ten-minute timer to melt the marshmallows covering the top.

"Sure did. It looks great," Dad responds. "It's very fitting of my little bookworm to create a library for this one."

"Is it great enough for you to call us the winners before the rest of them get here?" I flash Dad a wink, and he rolls his eyes at me.

"Too late, Big Sis, the winners have now arrived!" Phil comes boasting into the kitchen.

"You mean losers!" Piper yells from the hallway. "Austin and I will be taking home this win. Thank you very much!"

Just then, we all hear a loud crash in the dining room and go running.

Please don't be our library. Please, please, please don't be our library.

When we enter the dining room, Kevin is crouched over their ruined gingerbread creation, looking utterly defeated.

"No, no, NO!" Phil screams out, turning to Kevin. "What did you do?"

Kevin looks up at all of us. "I–I tripped over Little E. It was his fault!"

Phil glares at Little E. He's sitting on one of the dining chairs wearing a flannel sweater that matches Dad's, licking his paws like he has no cares in the world. He starts to stalk towards him. "That mother-fuc–"

"Oh no, you don't! Leave my boy alone!" Dad steps into his path and grabs the cat, cradling him like a baby. "He didn't mean it. Isn't that right, little buddy?" He pets Little E behind his ears, making him purr loudly over the deadly silence.

The door opens behind us, and I turn to see Spencer and his parents walk inside. Mrs. Larson is carrying a plate of cookies, and I smile when Spencer takes it out of her hands. He quickly kisses her cheek before disappearing into the kitchen with the baked goods.

"Oh dear, what did we miss?" Mrs. Larson's eyes widen as she takes in the gingerbread mess that used to be Phil and Kevin's—whatever it was.

Austin steps over the mess and greets his mom with a hug. "Kevin tripped over the cat and dropped the Eiffel Tower," he says sadly.

I shouldn't be secretly happy that Little E intervened, but I can't help it. I'm competitive to my core, and I know without a doubt that the Eiffel Tower would have won. Phil had always had a knack for making the best-looking gingerbread houses, and with Kevin's need for perfectionism, I knew theirs would have taken the prize. I peek over at the dining room table where Spencer left our library and sigh when I see ours is still intact.

Then I look over and see Piper's and Austin's, and my heart sinks.

They made the freaking Titanic—and it's freaking perfect.

I may be an adult, but there's nothing wrong with a good old pout session on the porch steps occasionally. I can't help it. I'm being a broody brat about the fact that we didn't win. But it's hard to argue with the judges when the Titanic was much better than ours. That doesn't mean I'm happy about it, though.

Our gingerbread library kicked ass. Plus, I saw a different side of Spencer while we brought it to life. He was patient, kind, and incredibly playful. He thinks I didn't notice how he purposely kept finding reasons to touch my hands or sneaking the candy off the bookshelves I was making and eating them. I noticed every time his eyes lingered on me. On my body.

It made me feel empowered and sexy like I never have before. Just being around Spencer makes me feel alive again. Not just this shell of a person trying to force myself to love a job I hate or to find beauty in a city that I despise living in. I don't want this feeling ever to go away, and I'm reluctant to be apart from him tonight. There's no real reason for me to go back with him and stay the night again, but I wish there were.

The front door opens behind me, and I expect it to be Spencer since he seems to know when these moods strike me. But I'm surprised to find that it's Kevin. I guess now is as good a time as any to have that much-needed talk with him, too.

Piper, Spencer, Kevin.

I have too many important conversations this Christmas, and I hate it. I've never been good with words. I'm much better at ignoring issues until they come full circle and blow up in my face, which isn't the most mature or healthy lifestyle.

"Hey, Pheebs. Can we talk?" Kevin asks from behind me.

I pat the spot next to me, inviting him to sit. Kevin wipes the small amount of snow and mud that cakes the steps before he sits down. Typical. He's never liked messy things. Maybe that's why he dumped me last year: I'm too messy.

Too emotional. Too pensive. Too stuck in my own thoughts, afraid to voice them.

"So, Spencer, huh?" He says casually.

I whip my head toward him, my eyes wide with surprise. I didn't think we were that obvious, but if Kevin has picked up on whatever this is, I can guarantee our families have, too. So now, if this ends badly, it'll affect everything. And that was the last thing I wanted.

I choose to play dumb instead. "What do you mean?" I make sure my face matches my confused tone.

By the knowing stare Kevin's shooting my way, I know he's not buying this for a minute.

"Are we that obvious?" I ask him, embarrassment flooding my body. I don't want to talk about this with Kevin. It's awkward. It's weird. It's uncomfortable. But maybe this is my chance to set the record straight between us for good.

He chuckles dryly. "You aren't obvious at all. In fact, I would have thought you hated the guy with how much you *don't* acknowledge him. Spencer, though, that guy can't keep his eyes off you." Kevin flashes me a small smile. "I wasn't sure until I watched him pass you the potatoes."

"The potatoes?" Now I'm really confused.

"You didn't pull away when he caressed your hand. I don't think anyone noticed, though. Just me," he says sadly.

This is what I didn't want. I may not want to be with Kevin, but I never wanted to hurt him.

"I'm sorry, Kev. I really am. This wasn't in the plans," I say, frustration clear in my tone. "I didn't mean for any of this to happen. I didn't even want to come home, let alone run into him again. And you showing up was most definitely not on my bingo card this year." He nods in understanding as I continue. "I think I've been in love with Spencer Larson since I was old enough to be interested in the opposite sex," I confess.

"We just...messed up somewhere along the way. I'm still not sure what's going on between us, but I didn't mean for you to watch whatever is happening right in front of you. I didn't think I'd ever see you again after we broke up."

I take a deep breath before continuing. "I'm not upset that you're here, though. It was a surprise, yes," I say. We both chuckle at that. "But I've missed you as a friend. I don't want to hurt you, but I have to be honest. I have loved watching you, Phil, and Pipes somewhat get along, and my parents obviously don't hate you anymore. Our relationship ended a year ago, and I'm not looking to rekindle it. What we had was fun, but it was also difficult. We have such different ideas in mind for our futures, and there isn't anything wrong with that," I sigh, peeking over at him. I'm glad when I see that smile still tugged on his lips. "We make much better friends than we ever did lovers."

Kevin blows out a long breath. "You're right. You're always right," he says. "I didn't come here to make drama. I need you to know that. A small part of me hoped we'd see each other again, and those sparks would fly between us again. I'm not upset that it didn't happen, though. I mostly came here because I wanted to apologize for how I ended things. You didn't deserve to be dumped that way. I can give you a million and one excuses, but seeing you so happy and vibrant and just...alive around your family. It broke something in me because I knew that wasn't a life I'd ever be able to give you," he confesses.

I already knew all of this because he told me earlier, but hearing it again after everything that's happened with Spencer is the closure I needed.

"I just want you to be happy, Pheebs. I've always wanted that. If this Spencer dude makes you happy, you need to figure out what's next between you. Don't let the fear of the past ruin what could possibly be that future you've always dreamed of." He knocks his shoulder softly into mine. "You know, the one with the happily ever after and the handful of kids and whatnot."

Now I'm full-blown crying. Happy tears, though. Kevin might be a dick sometimes, but he sure knows how to flip to being the sweetest and most understanding guy I've ever met. "Thank you, Kev. I really needed to hear that," I sniffle, and he rolls his eyes at me like he's always done when I cry over silly things.

He gets to his feet and holds his hand out to help me. "I guess I should take my heartbroken ass back to New York, huh?"

"No!" I startle us both with my loud objection. "I mean, you can't leave now. I need you to stay until the contest is over!"

He raises his eyebrow at me, a smirk playing on his lips. "You mean you need me to stay so you can have an excuse to stay partnered up with Mr. Spencey."

I flush red. "I didn't say that...but yes?"

Kevin laughs as he wraps me into a playful hug. He still smells like that expensive cologne, and I allow myself to breathe it in deeply, knowing this is both our goodbye as a couple and our hello as friends. "Honestly, I was hoping you'd say that," he admits. "Because I'm enjoying the hell out of pissing your brother off." We both laugh loudly, pulling out of each other's arms.

"And I can't wait to watch his face crumble when you beat him this year." He winks. "Plus, I may or may not have had a hand tipping the scales in your favor today. That is until the dynamic duo showed up with the freaking Titanic."

"Kevin! Tell me that you did not ruin your Eiffel Tower on purpose?"

His only response is to gesture to his lips, zip them closed and toss the invisible key behind his back.

The Mistletoe Feud 2023 Standings:

Task One: The Christmas Market Salesman
WINNER: PHOEBE

Task Two: Surviving the Snow-Fort
WINNER: PHIL & KEVIN

Task Three: The Battle of the Gingerbread
WINNER: PIPER & AUSTIN

Task Four:
WINNER:

Task Five:
WINNER:

CHAPTER TWENTY

Spencer

I was surprised when Phoebe asked if she could come again tonight. I'm even more surprised that we're sitting in strained silence on the ride there, though. I have a terrible feeling in my gut over whatever is on her mind, and part of it is due to my stupid snooping.

I couldn't help but notice when Phoebe and Kevin disappeared from the table after we all finished eating the fantastic meal Mrs. Andrews had cooked. They didn't stay long enough to hear the next task: the ugly sweater contest. I know how much Phoebe's always loved this task, and with her by my side, we're a shoo-in for the win. I couldn't wait to find Phoebe and tell her so we could start our plans as soon as possible.

That is until I saw her and Kevin cozied up and laughing together on the house's front steps. It's not my place to act all 'macho man' and try to stake a claim on Phoebe, but I'd be lying if I told you I wasn't sitting here sweating bullets while wondering what they talked about. Phoebe and I haven't exactly talked about the status of whatever this is between us. Seeing her and Kevin being all cute and chummy together makes me want to ask her and put a label on us.

Are we just friends?

Are we friends with benefits until she goes back to New York?

Are we taking the plunge and seeing if this can turn into something real?

The latter is what I'd be happiest with. Phoebe, however, may feel differently. I may be just a body to keep her warm and occupied until she and Kevin work their relationship out. And that stings more than I'd like to admit. I also feel like a jackass for feeling that way because I know we can't take this any further until I admit to her why I kissed Piper all those years ago. And I can't do that.

In other words, I'm knee-deep in crap and what-ifs.

It isn't long before I pull into the driveway, but I'm still wondering what's going on with Phoebe. It isn't the longest drive from her parent's house to mine, but it feels like hours of tense silence between us. I don't like it, but I'm unsure how to approach it.

Once I've parked and turned the truck off, neither of us moves to get out. I peer over at Phoebe and notice her gnawing on her bottom lip and tugging at her fingers like she's always done when nervous.

I reach over and place my hand over hers. "Talk to me, Pheebs," I tell her. "I can tell something is eating at you. Whatever it is, you can tell me. We can work through it together."

She moves her hand and intertwines her fingers with my own. "Umm, I need to ask you something, and I feel really stupid for bringing it up. So please bear with me." Her voice is low, and I can see her chest rising and falling in rapid rhythm. She's nervous. "It's going to sound dumb, especially this many years later." I instantly freeze. I know exactly what she's about to ask, and I have no idea how I'm going to be able to answer it.

I know this is the end of us.

Phoebe squeezes my hand tighter. "I have to know why you asked me to be your date to the Winter Formal, just to kiss Piper hours later." Her grip on my hand is unyielding. I don't think either of us are breathing. "I know it seems silly. Believe me, Spencer. I feel like the biggest idiot bringing this up now, especially after how wonderful the last couple of days have been with you. But, if we decide this is something real, something with a future, I really need to know why."

Her beautiful green eyes are pleading with me, her expression nervous but hopeful. Completely unaware that I'm about to ruin it all.

I wrap my other hand around hers, cradling it between my palms. I bring her hand to my lips and place what I know will be my last kiss onto her skin. "Phoebe, I have loved every moment I've spent with you these last few days. This time together was a gift I never expected, and I hope you know how much I care about you.

About us." She smiles fondly at me, and it breaks my heart. "I feel like I've waited my whole life for you to come back, to give me a second chance. Whenever I passed a girl with red hair like yours in the streets, I would instantly do a double take—hoping, praying, begging that it was you. When I saw you at the airport, you took my breath away. You're even more beautiful than you were as a kid, and getting to know you all over again over these last couple of days has been one of the biggest pleasures of my life." I pause to clear my throat, and she runs her fingers back and forth over my palm. "I need you to know that it's always been you. I need you to believe that, Phoebe." Her hand stills, and her body tenses. "And I'm sorry. But I can't tell you why I kissed Piper. It's just not my place."

For one idiotic moment, I hope she'll believe everything I've just told her and possibly be okay with leaving the past in the past.

But that hope withers away like a dandelion in the wind when she yanks her hand from mine.

"Take me home, Spencer," Phoebe says cooly. It's almost as if her heart has turned to stone, and instead of turning into a crying mess, she's just turned off any feelings she has for me altogether.

"Please, try to understand. If I could tell you, I would do so in a heartbeat. I swear I would. But it's not my secret to tell. What I can tell you is that my heart belongs to you. It's always been yours, Phoebe," I plead with her.

She refuses to look my way again, refuses to listen. And I can't even blame her. I knew this would be the spark that lit the flame and that this omission would only bring total and utter destruction to us.

"Take. Me. Home."

I sigh, acknowledging that this is it. I can't keep this secret without losing her, and I can't tell Phoebe without hurting Piper in the process.

The drive back to her house is quiet, unlike the screaming in my heart for letting it come to this.

For losing her again.

The colorful Christmas lights around her house give her silhouette a festive glow, but the anger radiating off her is nothing but. She doesn't leave the truck immediately but hasn't spoken during the drive here. She's been on her phone, scrolling social media or possibly texting. I don't know. I just know that she's furious with me. I've tried wrapping my head around any excuse to give her to make her change her mind, but it's useless.

There isn't anything I can do without hurting everyone involved.

"Wait here," Phoebe says curtly as she exits the truck, slamming the door angrily behind her.

"Yes, ma'am," I mutter, knowing she won't hear me. I've seen her upset and happy, but this might be the first time I've seen her angry. She's a force to be reckoned with, stomping her way to the front door and throwing it open in an irritated fashion.

A few minutes later, the front door opens, and Piper steps out. She's bundled up in a dark green winter coat and wearing the most ridiculous bright yellow beanie. She looks like she just stepped out of a Packers game. She shoots me a look that screams, 'You done messed up, Spencey,' as she walks up to the truck and enters the passenger seat.

My heart drops when I realize that Phoebe isn't going to come back out, even if it's what I wholly deserve.

"Sup, Spence," Piper happily greets me. "I've come equipped with a list of craft items and an earful of Phoebe's rage. Which should we discuss first?" She flashes me a smug smile and reaches into her bright yellow purse, pulling out a small notepad.

"I guess we can talk while we shop. Where to?" I sigh, putting the truck in gear and driving away from the house.

"Hobby Lobby, I guess. Pheebs gave us a list of supplies she needs you to get for the ugly sweater contest," Piper says as I drive down the main road, taking a left past the Christmas market and heading towards the small shopping center in Noelsville.

Our town isn't tiny, but it's not large either. We've got most convenience stores and plenty of fast food chains to pick from. The best part about this town is the small-town feel. Everyone knows everyone, and everyone greets each other with a smile. Most locals try their best to shop at the Mom & Pop shops over the larger chain stores. However, Hobby Lobby is the go-to craft store in town, located only a few miles from the town center. We pull into the crowded parking lot and head inside.

It's like Christmas threw up in here. There are decorations of every kind just waiting to be purchased and taken home. The entire store smells like those cinnamon-infused pinecones, which now remind me of Phoebe and our Fireball night.

"Cheer up, Romeo. She won't stay mad forever. Grab a cart, and let's get this over with. I have a date with Mom's homemade apple pie," Piper teases. "Now, tell me what you did to piss off my sister. I've never seen her this angry. And you know she's always been the moody twin," she remarks, raising her eyebrows at me. "So, spill it."

I push the cart through several aisles to find one that isn't flooded with shoppers. I steer us towards the back of the store, where the crowd is thinnest, and stop in front of a row of frames. "Phoebe is pissed at me because she asked why I kissed you during the Winter Formal," I admit, blowing out a breath of frustration.

"Oh." Piper's eyes go wide as she stares at me. "Did...did you tell her?"

I give her a look of indignation. "Of course, I didn't. I wouldn't do that to you," I promise her.

She yanks her bright yellow beanie off of her head and throws it into her giant bag. "Well, crap. This puts a damper on my whole 'if you hurt my sister, I'll cut your nads off' talk," Piper chuckles. "This is all my fault, Spencer. I promise I'll fix this."

She's gnawing on her bottom lip like Phoebe does when nervous or upset.

"Don't worry about it, Pipes. Phoebe and I just aren't written in the stars," I pause, forcing myself to accept what I've just admitted to her. "And that's okay."

Piper stomps her foot loudly and throws her hands onto the cart, making me jump. "No, it's not! None of this is okay. You and Phoebe are soulmates. We've both known it for years. I'll talk to her. I'll fix this. You both shouldn't have to suffer just because I'm a coward," she exclaims. "It's about time for my family to know the real me anyway, right?"

A small, nervous smile plays on her lips, but I know she's an anxious mess on the inside.

I reach over and ruffle her hair, and she yelps in protest. "Pipes, I'd never forgive myself if you got hurt because of all this, too. So don't force yourself to do anything you're not ready for. Promise me?"

She quickly puts her short, dark hair back into place. "I promise. Even if I don't come clean to my entire family, I swear I'll talk to Phoebe. Pinky promise." She holds her pinky out, and we both settle into comfortable companionship after I've sealed the promise by wrapping my pinky up with hers.

Phoebe may have my heart, but Piper will always be my best friend.

"What does your sister have on that list? We don't have much time between now and the next judging." Piper shows me the list, and I'm relieved it doesn't have many items.

A white crew neck sweater in my size and one in Phoebe's. Grey and green garment dye, darker gray yarn, gold spray paint, large sequins in multiple colors, lightweight rocks in assorted sizes, a sewing kit, and some type of adhesive that must be safe for clothing.

I'm not sure what she has planned, but Piper has already told me Phoebe doesn't want my help whatsoever. Mr. Andrews has a small block party scheduled for tomorrow at noon, and of course, the theme is 'Ugly Sweaters Are Better.' There'll be a contest for everyone to join, and then there will be a separate contest for The Mistletoe Feud later tomorrow evening. I've been instructed to show up before the party begins so Phoebe can get me into my sweater and make whatever last-minute tweaks she needs to.

I'd rather her get me out of my sweater, but my life is obviously not a Hallmark movie.

CHAPTER TWENTY-ONE

Phoebe

Once Piper comes home with the craft supplies, I lock myself in my 'not-room' and get to work. I don't want to talk to her right now. I love her, and I owe her some one-on-one time. But that will have to wait another day because right now, I know she'll try to get me to stop being angry at Spencer and give him another chance.

And I'm nowhere near ready to do that.

So, instead, I'll work through the night on these epic ugly sweaters and blast my music, pointedly ignoring the whole world just for tonight. I've dyed both sweaters: gray for Spencer and green for myself. I had already planned on making this sweater for myself, but after my fight with Spencer, it makes the one I'm creating much more fitting for him.

We may not win this one, but I don't care about the contest right now. I'm dressing for revenge tomorrow like the stone-cold Medusa I know I can be.

I've already sewn on the sequins I needed for my sweater, making it look like some technicolored snake skin. The only thing left I need for myself is my headband. I gather my supplies and make my way to the backyard. I have to spray paint all these plastic snakes I brought so I can finally put my headpiece together. I'm praying it comes out the way I've pictured it in my head ever since I told Piper I was coming home for Christmas.

Because it's going to be freaking epic.

I can't wait to see Spencer's face when he sees his sweater tomorrow. My petty side hopes that he hates it as much as I hate that he won't tell me the truth.

How hard is it for him to admit that he wanted Piper? After spending the last couple of days together, I don't think he wants her anymore, but I'll never be able to be sure until he tells me that.

He's said that he cares for me and wants me just as much as I want him.

Why can't he tell me that he doesn't want her anymore? I know I'm being stupid, but I need to hear it from his lips. I *need* to hear that he may have liked her back then but feels nothing in the romantic department toward her anymore. I can't give him my all, knowing I'll always have that Piper-sized bird on my shoulder reminding me that I'm the backup option.

When I come inside after spray painting my snakes, I run into Phil and Piper in the kitchen.

And suddenly, everything with Spencer seems silly and stupid.

When was the last time I had both of my siblings in one room at the same time?

When was the last time we spent time together, and wasn't it over a group Facetime call?

Why am I letting a boy ruin the little time we have together this week?

This is me, vowing to be a better sister because I have missed them both so much, and I'm tired of being the moody little rain cloud that I've been today.

"Hey guys," I greet them with a smile. "What are you two up to?" I lean against the marble countertop and snag the cookie that Phillip was about to eat. Smirking at him, I shoved the whole thing in my mouth.

"Well, I was about to enjoy Mrs. Larson's last pumpkin-chocolate chip cookie," he pouts. "But there's this person named Phoebe who must share some DNA with the cookie monster." He laughs loudly at his stupid joke, making Piper and I roll our eyes at each other.

Piper crosses the kitchen and wraps her arms around me, laying her head on my shoulder while we watch Phil dig around in the gnome-shaped cookie jar we've lovingly named Gnomeo. He flashes me a smug smile when he pulls out half a gingerbread man from Nana's. The little weasel knows that those are my favorite.

"How do you guys feel about going out and doing something fun? Just us three," I ask while trying to swipe the cookie from Phil again. He's prepared this time, though, and easily dodges my attack.

He shoves the cookie into his mouth. "What did you have in mind?" Phil asks with his mouth full—such a turd.

I shrug my shoulders. "I don't know. I just came inside and realized we hadn't done anything with the three of us in years. I figured it might be a good night to change that."

Piper squeezes me tighter. "I love that idea, Pheebs. How about we go to the Christmas market? None of us have gone there just for fun yet, right? And I could use a cup of spiked eggnog. We can get you two some more cookies too! Oh, and I need to get Mom and Dad a Christmas gift!" She yells excitedly.

Phil shrugs and heads towards the front door to grab his coat. "Why not? Let's go!"

I've always loved coming to the Christmas market at night. The lights on every little hut shine brightly, giving off that whole Whoville vibe throughout the town square. They also put smaller trees throughout the market, all decorated and lit up, adding to the festive atmosphere.

"I wish you guys could see a Christmas market in Germany. They go all out," Piper says wistfully. "They call their markets *Weihnachtsmärkte*, and they are truly something out of a fairytale. Each year, they make custom mugs with the market name and year, and when you buy a mug of hot chocolate or *Glühwein,* you get to keep the mug. Last year, my dorm mates and I went to four different markets, and each was even better than the last one."

"What's *Glühwein?*" I ask Piper.

Her eyes light up as she explains that it's a warm, spiced wine they sell during the holiday season in Germany and most other European countries. It sounds wonderful, and I could use a glass of something warm to help fight the chill in the air tonight.

"Sounds like us Americans need to get on board with this spiced alcohol thing because it's cold as balls out here tonight!" Phil wraps his black winter coat tighter around him and blows into his hands. "Let's get some hot chocolate and find a warm place to hang while we figure out what to get Mom and Dad for Christmas."

The three of us head towards Santa's Eggnog Hut, happily surprised that the line is short. Most booths here have lines that wrap around each little vendor's hut. Many people don't realize that Santa's Eggnog Hut also sells the best hot chocolate. It's a well-kept secret from the locals, so we can skip the lines and get a mug quickly.

Once we all have our drink of choice, we browse each of the small booths. Piper gets one of her friends an ornament with the town square painted on it. Phil grabs some more gingerbread cookies from Nana's and some homemade fudge from Terry's Fudge Shop to go along with them. I head over to Conrad's Rad Ornaments, unsure what I'm looking for, but I know when I see it.

He's made the Iron Throne using his wood-burning tools.

It's painted silver with accents of white and black to make the swords pop out more. He's added a shiny glossy over it, making it look like the throne from the show. I gasp when I see it and pick it up carefully.

"My daughter loves that show," Mr. Conrad laughs gruffly from behind the counter.

"She's got good taste," I respond warmly. "It's a great show, and this is one of the best ornaments I've seen you make." We smile at each other as I bring the ornament to the counter to pay. He has another small tree sitting at the counter, decorated with more of the ornaments he's made. An ugly laugh escapes my lips when I see a hot dog ornament hanging from the smaller tree, and I pull it off gently. "I'll take this one too, please."

"The Iron Throne and a hot dog," he chuckles, shaking his head. "Strange combination you got here."

"It's an inside joke with a—friend," I tell him, praying he can't hear my heart cracking from his side of the desk. I hand him my debit card, and he hands it back with both ornaments carefully wrapped up. "Thank you. I hope you have a great rest of your night, Mr. Conrad."

"You too, hun. Tell your Pop I said hello, and I'm counting down the days until we can go on a fishing trip again!" His laughter follows me as I walk further into the market, looking for my siblings.

I find them at the caricature artist's booth, and I know exactly what they're thinking when they wave me over to take a seat behind the easel.

"Okay, should we be merpeople? Or riding giant turtles?" Phil asks as I sit down.

"I told you we should be little elves!" Piper smacks his arm playfully.

I look at the artist's designs hanging around the booth, and a rueful smile paints my face when my eyes land on a cat one. "No, we are going to be cats dressed in matching sweaters, and we can have Little E painted on one of our laps. Can you do that?" I ask the artist. He tells me he can. "The cat needs to be gray, and he has to have a sweater that matches the rest of ours."

Phil high-fives me, and Piper squeezes my arm. "This might be the best gift idea we've ever had. Dad is going to flip!" Phil exclaims excitedly.

"And Mom is going to be thrilled to have an updated photo of all her kids together," Piper chuckles.

I hold my smile as the artist does his thing, but my mind is stuck on the stupid ornaments I have wrapped in my bag. And the guy I *shouldn't* want to give them to.

The guy I shouldn't be dying to see again tomorrow.

CHAPTER TWENTY-TWO

Spencer

Instead of moping around the house after I dropped Piper off at home, I hit up one of my favorite watering holes: Blarney's Pub. The owner, Pat, is a beast of an Irish man, adorned with fiery red hair and a beard that he likes to decorate in different braids. He pours a wicked Guinness, and his fried food is perfection.

Nothing quite smooths over a self-induced broken heart like a platter of fried onion rings and the juiciest fried mushrooms.

I take my usual seat at the end of the bar, drinking and eating in silence while watching the Panthers vs. the Packers game, when someone pulls the stool out from next to me and takes a seat. The bar is nearly empty, and I'm already in a foul mood. As I turn to ask the interloper to move down a bit, I'm met with the smug, smiling face of Kevin.

He calls the bartender over, orders a Guinness, and then snags one of my onion rings from my plate.

"Look, Bacon, I'm not in the mood for your shit right now," I say in the most annoyed tone I can muster up, making sure he knows that I don't want him here.

"Bacon? Really? That's the best you can come up with? Weak sauce, dude. Weak. Sauce." He wiggles his eyebrows before shoving *my* onion ring into his mouth.

I roll my eyes and ignore him rather than fall into whatever baiting tactics he's trying to pull on me. Like I said, my mood is not up for company tonight, especially from this fancy coat-wearing jackass.

He reaches over to swipe another onion ring, and I slap his hand away like he's an errant child who needs scolding.

"Come on, dude. Lighten up," Kevin says as he shoves my shoulder.

"What part of I don't want company did you not understand? I figured some big-money pants douchebag like you would have some higher education. Therefore, you should understand the words coming from my mouth." I shoot him a dirty look and take a swig of my beer, letting the stout slide down my throat so I don't pummel the man.

He chuckles lightly next to me. "You should be thanking me."

Dammit, I bite. "What do you mean?"

Kevin takes his beer from Pat and offers thanks before taking a long swig. It's taking every ounce of self-control not to grab the draft and chuck it across the room so that he'll answer me. "Alright, alright, chill, man," he says as soon as he sets his draft back on the bar top. "I take it you and Phoebe got in a fight if you're sitting here this pissy. Am I right?"

I grunt out a non-committal response. I don't want to talk to him about Phoebe. I don't want to talk to anyone *but* Phoebe.

I refrain from swatting his hand away when he reaches over and plucks a fried mushroom off my plate.

Kevin smirks at me again before dipping the mushroom into my ranch. I force myself to take a deep, calming breath before I do something I'll regret, like breaking his nose. I slide my plate over to him and take another long pull of my beer before motioning to Pat that I need another.

"I'll take your silence as a yes," Kevin jokes. "I'm telling you right now, Spence. You better fix whatever you did wrong. A girl like Phoebe won't come around twice in this lifetime, and I don't want you to end up like me. Alone and regretting not figuring out how to fix it sooner. Right?" He tips his beer in my direction, and I begrudgingly clink my draft with his.

I sigh, picking at the plate of food between us. "I don't think I can fix this one," I admit.

"Bullshit. Whatever it is, it's fixable. Look at me. I dumped Phoebe in front of her entire family because I freaked out thinking that I couldn't be saddled down with that kind of lifestyle." I raise an eyebrow at him in confusion, and he throws his hands up in frustration. "You know the life she wants. The big blue house with the perfect decorations. A husband who comes home on time every night and kisses her and the kids hello before sitting down for a home-cooked meal. I won't ever be that person, and that's what she'll always want."

He flashes me a smile that doesn't quite reach his dark eyes. "You could give her that life. All you need to do is pull that giant head out of the clouds and make it happen. I've seen the way you look at her, and I know you care for her more than either of you let on. So, whatever it is getting in the way, you have to find a way around it. Don't lose her over something stupid."

I want to argue with him, but what's the point? He's not entirely wrong, even if that situation isn't as easy as fixing it. Piper has to tell Phoebe everything on her terms, which I cannot force her into. The fact that she's already offered to tell Phoebe is a huge deal. I won't mess that moment up for her just because I miss Phoebe not looking at me with disdain in her eyes.

For now, I'll sit here, drinking my sorrows away with the most unlikely of allies. Bacon might not be such a bad guy, even if he dresses like a rich douchebag and keeps eating all the best-looking onion rings on my plate.

"How are you so cool with giving advice to another man who wants the same woman as you?" I ask him, curious to hear his answer.

He waves Pat over and orders two Irish car bombs before turning back to me. "Because I love her enough to want her to be happy. She wasn't happy with the lifestyle we lived together. I know that now. Seeing her at home, in her element, reminded me of the woman she was when we met. She was radiant and full of life. A few years under my thumb dulled that light in her," Kevin tells me as he picks at the label on his empty bottle. "You know what they say about how some people just bring out the worst in each other? Phoebe brought out the best in me, and I grabbed onto that feeling with no regard for how poorly I was treating her in return. I focused so hard on what I wanted that I turned her into a shell of the happy person she was when I met her. You brought the light back."

Pat returns with two more drafts of Guinness and two shots of Bailey's mixed with whiskey. Kevin picks up his shot glass and hands me the other. "Bottoms up, Spence!" Then we both drop the shot glass into the Guinness and chug as quickly as possible before it curdles.

Not a bad way to nurse a self-induced broken heart, not a bad way at all.

The next day I make sure to show up at the Andrews' house early like I promised. I'm immediately met with a hug from Mrs. Andrews, then steered to the dining room and given a plate of chocolate chip pancakes and the crispiest bacon I've ever had. Kevin comes out of the kitchen moments later wearing a Santa apron and a Santa hat perched over his annoyingly tousled dark locks.

"Best bacon you've ever had, right?" He wags his eyebrows at me, and I find myself not wanting to punch his lights out. Maybe that's how friendships are made: three Irish car bombs and bonding over more fried food than we could eat.

I take another bite of the bacon, relishing in the maple after-taste of it. "'Tis pretty good, my dude," I tell him after I chew. "But I wouldn't expect anything less from you, Bacon." I tip my head at him in thanks, and we eat the rest of our meal together. It's a refreshing change of pace, not hating the guy. I was a little worried that seeing him today might be awkward without all the liquor to wash away the angst between us, but everything seems okay this morning. I don't know if I'd call him a friend, but I don't hate having him around.

How could I hate someone who only wants Phoebe to be happy?

"You seen her yet?" Kevin asks over his cup of coffee. I shake my head, and the overwhelming grip of fear grasps me by the throat. I haven't seen her since she got out of the truck yesterday, and I'm nervous to be in the same room as her today. "Well, if it makes you feel better, she seems to be in high spirits this morning. Why don't you try to talk to her? She's in her room." Kevin stands up, takes my empty plate, and disappears into the kitchen again.

"You're a real weirdo, Bacon," I shout to him before following his advice and heading up the stairs to find Phoebe.

I need to get my ugly sweater on anyway, so I might as well rip this bandaid off quickly. I knock quietly on Phoebe's door; at least, I think it's still her door. I'm not sure if the Andrews have moved around rooms since all the kids have now moved out.

When she opens the door, I'm momentarily stunned to see she's only wearing a pair of high-waisted jeans and a fancy, lace purple bra.

I run my eyes up and down her body before I realize what a perv I must look like, and I avert my eyes quickly. "Umm, sorry...I was just uh...coming for my sweater," I blurt out, sounding like the biggest idiot ever.

Phoebe giggles softly. "Come on, it's not like you haven't seen it before," she teases playfully.

Wait. Is she not still angry at me? Hope blossoms in my chest. Maybe Piper has talked to her already.

"Don't worry, I'm still pissed at you," Phoebe says over her shoulder. "But I could use your help getting this sweater over my hair."

And just like that, the small boom of hope withers away.

I step into the room and close the door quietly behind me. When I turn, I see that much hasn't changed in this room from the last time I saw it. Little E has a giant cat tree hanging out near the window, and a few storage totes are stacked in the corner. The rest look like they didn't dare touch a thing after Phoebe left five years ago. The walls are still that same deep shade of purple, and all of Phoebe's awards and photos are lined around the white vanity mirror. Her bed comforter matches the curtains, which both have black cats printed all over them.

I watch as Phoebe works on finishing her makeup in front of the mirror. She grabs two sweaters from the small closet, hands one to me, and tosses the other on the bed. When our fingers accidentally graze each other, I feel the same electric shock that I've always felt around her. All I want to do is get on my knees and beg for her forgiveness. Beg her to take me back and let me hold her, kiss her, share my life with her.

Her eyes are hooded when they meet mine, and I wonder if she feels the same pang of desire I'm feeling for her now. Her blazing red hair curls wildly around her face, and the green eyeshadow she's used makes her eyes pop even brighter than usual. Her deep burgundy lipstick gives her a mysteriously sexy and haunted look, and my insides ache to be nearer to her. To be able to touch her. To hear those lips screaming my name again as she comes around my fingers.

I feel myself straining in my jeans, and I mentally chastise myself, forcing myself to stop thinking about her naked and instead help her get ready for the next task.

"Can you help me get this around my head without ruining my hair too much?" Phoebe asks, pulling me out of my thoughts and back to the present. "I should have put it on first, but it's so hot in this house today, with Mom and Kevin cooking nonstop."

I take the mess of green sequined fabric, carefully navigate it over her curls, and pull it away from her face so her makeup doesn't get smeared. Once it's entirely on, she turns and gives me a shy smile while she runs her hands down the front of the sweater, fixing errant sequins and patting them back into place. She looks like a mermaid, with red hair and seductive red lips. Maybe she's a siren after my heart.

"Are you supposed to be a mermaid?" I ask skeptically.

She shakes her head and laughs. "Nope, but let's get yours on, and maybe you'll understand." Phoebe picks up the gray sweater she threw on the bed, and I notice it has what looks like stones glued all over it.

"Shirt off, Spencer," Phoebe says playfully.

I shrug my jacket off and pull the black v-neck I'm wearing over my head, tossing them onto her bed. I reach out to grab the sweater from Phoebe, but she seems frozen in place while staring at my bare chest. I smirk at her as I step closer, grabbing my sweater from her hand and pulling it over my head.

It's like wearing a weighted vest. A bulky, stone-covered, weighted vest.

I turn to look at myself in the small vanity mirror when I notice Phoebe reaching into the closet again. She pulls on a headpiece that has sticks protruding in every direction. Turning around, I see they aren't sticks—they're golden plastic snakes.

"Phoebe," I say incredulously. "Did you turn yourself into Medusa so I could be the poor soul you turned into stone with your unearthly beauty?" I raise an eyebrow at her, looking at her sweater and then down at mine. She covers her mouth with her hands and silently laughs while nodding yes to my question.

I can't believe this woman, and I don't think I've loved her more than I do right now. This hilarious over-the-top 'I'm pissed at you, Spencer' gesture. It's incredible, really. If these sweaters don't win, then our parents must have zero sense of humor.

But even if we don't win, I still feel like the biggest winner for getting her riled up enough to do something this epic. Phoebe has always won the ugly sweater contest, and it's because she has always treated it like a costume contest. In contrast, everyone else has just bought the most ridiculous sweater at Walmart or one of the other chain stores in Noelsville. Phoebe has always handmade her own, and she certainly outdid herself this time.

Phoebe tells me it's time to go downstairs to help set up for the party, and before she does, she pauses at the door and hisses at me. Actually, hisses *at* me.

My wicked little Medusa has jokes. Now I need to find something to make her laugh as hard as I am over being turned to stone.

CHAPTER TWENTY-THREE

Phoebe

"Is there a universe in existence that would allow me to just turn my heart off? Because if there is, I would like to go there for Christmas," I say to Piper as I sip my second spiked eggnog. We joke that eggnog is for the oldies, but the more I drink it, the more the taste grows on me. Maybe it's because I've eaten nothing today except for a couple strips of Kevin's crispy bacon or the fact that I'm feeling just a tad bit tipsy. Whatever the reason, I cannot keep my traitorous eyes off of my sexy stone man.

Well, not *my* sexy stone man.

But he could be if I could fly to that magic universe and turn off the feelings of self-doubt and uneasiness that have flooded my veins ever since our 'fight.' Why can't I just trust him when he says he wants me? Not Piper, *me*.

Spencer saunters to us and hands me a plate of honey-smoked ham, mashed potatoes, and two deviled eggs on the side. I'm so hungry, I could kiss him. And I secretly love that he knows deviled eggs are my favorite holiday food. I could eat an entire carton full of them, but it still wouldn't be enough to satisfy me.

I shove a whole one into my mouth and mumble 'thank you' through my overly full mouth. Spencer and Piper laugh at me, making my egg-filled smile even bigger. It's like having an orange slice in your mouth, except mine is all egg.

"Dude, you're disgusting!" Piper howls loudly. "Thank goodness you found a guy willing to kiss you," she jokes.

Spencer and I make eye contact, and I feel the red-hot blaze of a blush rush to my cheeks. I hold back a smile when I see Spencer's cheeks also turn a little rosy.

"Why, hello to my two favorite humans in this tiny town of Noelsville. How's the make-up session going?" Kevin puts his arms heavily around Spencer and me. I can smell the rum on his breath and can tell he's on the not-so-fun side of drunk by the way his hand keeps twitching on my shoulder. Some people get red cheeks. Some get talkative. Kevin gets twitchy.

Spencer claps Kevin loudly on his back. "I can see your sabotaging is working just perfectly," Spencer laughs, and we all look over as he points at Phil standing in the food line. His ugly sweater is downright ugly—in the wrong way. It's neon orange, and it looks like they've glued some tinsel around his chest.

"What is that sweater supposed to be?" Piper finally asks after we all stare at it for a beat.

Spencer and Kevin start laughing like they are in on some joke that the rest of us aren't privy to. Kevin clears his throat and grips my shoulder tighter, pulling me closer to him. "Well, Meduuuussaa," he drags out. "We turned dear Phillip into Ms. Tinsel Tits. Can't you tell?"

Piper throws her hand over her mouth, holding in what I'm sure is another bout of ugly laughter. "How did you talk him into that?"

Kevin releases Spencer and me, moves to where he's facing all three of us, and waves his hands over himself.

"What are we supposed to be looking at?" I ask because he's wearing a neon yellow sweater with nothing on it.

"It's supposed to say 'Santa's Balls,' but I never got around to putting it together," he says with a wink at Spencer. "We were supposed to show up as Tinsel Tits and Santa's Balls, but now it's just Phil looking like a Yeti's worst nightmare, walking around with those shiny, hairy tits. It's a travesty, really. Phillip will never meet a nice girl looking like that."

Kevin is officially drunk, and I pat him on the back before fetching the poor guy some water. When he drinks too much, he gets twitchy and starts trying to hook everyone up with somebody. We've got to sober him up before he starts marching around like the drunken matchmaker of Noelsville. But that was the side of him I fell in love with, so even though we're done in the relationship department, it's very nice to see his playful side come back out.

I run into Austin at the beverage table and notice his sweater wrapped weirdly on his body, almost like half of it is hanging off. "Austin, what is your sweater supposed to be?" I ask him as I dig through the ice chest for a water bottle.

"I can answer that!" Piper's sing-songy voice says from behind us.

Austin turns and smiles brightly at her and then puts his soda back on the table. "You ready?" He asks Piper. I watch in fascination as she climbs into the baggy part of his sweater and pops her head out from a hole I didn't notice before. Her arm slides through the second sleeve; before I know it, they are both wearing the same sweater.

I shake my head and giggle when they raise their hands like they're doing spirit fingers.

"That is actually sort of amazing," I tell them through my laughter.

Austin beams at me. "Thanks, only $39.99 at Target." He and Piper high-five each other across their massive joint body. "Too bad someone decided to go all out and is totally going to beat us this round. Your sweater is epic, Pheebs. I can't believe you had time to make both yours and my brothers in one night."

"Phoebe has always been a superstar with crafts. I expected nothing less from my little sister," Piper chimes in with a hint of genuine pride in her voice. "But we are winning the next one and taking the Mistletoe crown!"

They high-five each other again and then walk away in some weird choreographed crab walk.

"Alright, folks, it's time for the Ugly Sweater contest judging!" Dad yells loudly over the crowd. "Everyone participating, head up to Larson's driveway so we can get this thing started!"

Spencer meets me halfway, and I hiss at him playfully, moving my head so my snakes wiggle around. He freezes in place with a terrified expression on his face and his arms held over his head. A smile paints my lips when he flashes a wink at me before returning his body to normal.

"We got this one in the bag, Pheebs," Spencer smirks, holding his arm out for me. I snake my arm through his, relishing in his warmth and the scents of cinnamon and evergreen that seem to always radiate off his skin.

I hate that I've accidentally fallen for Spencer-freaking-Larson.

Later that night, our families sat around the giant bonfire we had put together in Larson's backyard. We're fully equipped with everything we need to make s'mores, and Mrs. Larson has Christmas music playing softly on the Bluetooth speaker near the back porch.

Today was nearly perfect.

Spencer and I won the ugly sweater contest and haven't fought again. Though, I guess it's not fair to call it a fight. I asked him a question—one he refused to answer. So, now we are at this weird standstill in whatever this relationship thing is. Was?

All I want to do is sit beside him on the other side of the fire, grab his hand, and disappear together for some alone time. The heated looks we've both been giving each other are torturous.

I want him. *I want him badly.*

"Just go over there already," Piper nudges me and motions towards Spencer. Apparently, our heated glances aren't as subtle as I thought they were.

"I can't, Pipes."

She scoffs at my answer. "What's stopping you? You've both been in love with each other for, like, a billion years. And now, you're both finally able to act on it. What's the problem?"

I bite my lip and stare nervously into the fire. I didn't want to have this talk with her, but I guess it's about time I act like an adult. I blow out a steadying breath. "You. You are the problem," I whisper to her. I feel like the worst sister in the world when I feel her body stiffen next to mine.

Instead of responding to me, she grabs my hand and tugs me up from my seat.

"Come on, we need to talk," Piper says quietly. "Pheebs and I are going to have a twin night. We will see you all in the morning for the next task!"

I barely have time to wave goodbye to anyone before she drags me out of the backyard and towards her car. "Piper, where are we going? We've both been drinking. It's a dumb idea to drive right now."

She unlocks the car and gets into the driver's seat. I momentarily debate going back into the house and leaving her to make stupid decisions alone, but I reluctantly get into the passenger's side. She slams the key into the ignition and fires up the car. Then she turns the headlights off, reclines her seat all the way back, and opens the shade for the sunroof.

I don't say anything as I follow suit until I'm reclined onto my back. We both gaze at the stars from the comfort of her heated car.

We lay in silence for an impossibly long time. I even glance over at Piper to make sure she didn't fall asleep on me, but her eyes are wide open. "What's wrong, Pipes?"

She takes a few deep breaths and starts tugging on the hem of her coat like she's always done when nervous. That's one thing we both have in common—the nervous tugs. "I know why you're angry at Spencer," she finally says. "But none of it was his fault. Please believe me when I say that. None of it was his fault. It was mine."

I turn awkwardly in my seat to face her, and I grab her hand, squeezing it tight across the center console. "What do you mean it was your fault?"

My chest feels tight, and my heart is pounding so fast I feel as though it's moments from exploding out of my chest. We've never talked about Spencer kissing her. The first and only time we talked about it was when I walked in on them kissing at the Winter Formal. She told me he kissed her and that she had no part in wanting it. I never brought it up with Spencer because I was humiliated that he asked me to be his date when he obviously wanted my sister the entire time.

A tear escapes her eye, and I watch in silence as it rolls down her cheek and disappears into her hair.

"I—I asked him to lie to you, or I guess, to let me lie to you," Piper says after a minute. "It's all so stupid now that I look back on it, but even though I know it's stupid, I've still let him lie for me all this time because I'm a coward, Phoebe. I've lied to you and everyone about who I truly am for years. My entire life. And for what? Because I was afraid you guys would shun me? Be ashamed of me?" She's full-blown crying now, and I'm still confused as ever.

"Piper, we could never shun you. *I* could never shun you. You're half my heart, and I would be lost without you. You're my soul-mate, my twin. We're in that whole 'If I jump, you jump' thing for life. You know that, right?"

"I know. I know. Which is why this is going to sound so stupid, and I'm so sorry for lying to you this entire time. I can't stand by and watch what you and Spencer have be torn to shreds over *me*." She squeezes my hand harder, and I know in my gut that this is monumental for my sister. So I squeeze tighter, holding on for the both of us.

"Okay, so here goes," Piper says with gritted teeth. "Remember those girls that would bully the hell out of us in school? Well, at the dance, I overheard them talking about me in the bathroom. They didn't know I was in there, but what they were saying was horrible. They kept saying over and over again that they thought I was gay and that they were going to prove it and tell the whole school that I was a lesbian. I panicked. Mostly because I couldn't imagine you hearing it from them or for our parents to find out that way," Piper chokes out through the river of tears streaming down her beautiful face.

"So I ran from the bathroom, and as soon as I heard them leave, I ran right into Spencer. The mean girls were right in line at that stupid photobooth the school set up, laughing at me and pointing. I knew they would out me, so I did the only thing I could do. I grabbed Spencer, and I kissed him in front of everyone."

I inhale sharply at her words, unable to fully process everything she's revealing to me. *She* kissed *him*?

"Anyways, you walked in, and I knew I was the worst big sister ever. I knew how much you liked each other, but I was selfish. And I asked him to lie for me to keep my secret safe. Spencer is the greatest guy I've ever met. He agreed to lie, and he's kept that secret all these years. He agreed to say it was him so I wouldn't lose you. Phoebe, I cannot lose you, but I understand if you hate me and need time to process all this."

I'm angry, and I'm hurt. But mostly, I'm relieved, and I'm proud. So damn proud of my stupid big sister for being brave enough to admit this all now. I know this isn't easy for her. Admitting to your family that your sexuality is not what we all assumed it was—well, that takes guts.

I pull my hand out of Piper's and get out of the car, walking around until I'm at Piper's door. I yank it open and motion her to get out, and as soon as her door is closed behind her, I wrap her into the biggest freaking hug imaginable.

"Piper, I'm so proud of you and honored that you shared this with me. It all makes so much sense now. All the anime lady posters on the walls and the serious lack of boy talk. I really should have guessed it years ago," I joke. "Thank you for trusting me. I love you, and I forgive you."

Another sob wracks her body. "You do? You forgive me?"

"Of course I do. You were a kid, and I wouldn't have been smart enough to throw them off like that. Do I hate that it had to be Spencer on our first date? Yes, I hate that. But none of that matters now because now neither of you has to lie to me about it," I pull her back so I can look at her. "And now I don't have to worry about the guy I'm sort of crushing on being hung up on my twin sister!"

We both hug some more and laugh even harder.

"Would you actually be up for some twin-only time? Because I'm seeing someone back in Germany, and she's supposed to Face-time me tonight. I'd love to introduce you to her if that'd be okay?" Piper's voice is full of hope and happiness, which I never realized was missing until now.

I link my arm with hers and steer us towards the house. "I would absolutely love to meet her. My stone-man can spend one more night in agony for making me think he wanted to date my sister this entire time. This seems like an acceptable punishment until I'm ready to jump his bones tomorrow."

That realization washes over me, and I want to sing from the rooftops because I'm so thrilled and ecstatic. The weight on my chest that told me I wasn't enough for Spencer and wasn't *who* he wanted vanished.

Spencer Larson really does want *me*.

The Mistletoe Feud 2023 Standings:

Task One: The Christmas Market Salesman
WINNER: PHOEBE

Task Two: Surviving the Snow-Fort
WINNER: PHIL & KEVIN

Task Three: The Battle of the Gingerbread
WINNER: PIPER & AUSTIN

Task Four: Ugly Sweaters Make Life Better
WINNER: PHOEBE & SPENCER

Task Five:
WINNER:

CHAPTER TWENTY-FOUR

Spencer

When I wake up the following day, I lay in bed and contemplate how to get Phoebe back for the 'stone-man' thing. Seeing her laugh and giggle whenever I froze in place after she hissed at me was honestly the best part of my day. That playful, jubilant side of her rarely tends to come out, so it's truly something special when it does.

I would sell my soul to see her smile every day—to live with her in pure happiness and contentment every single day.

There isn't much time between now and the start of the final task, whatever it may be, but I can't help but wrap my brain into knots trying to come up with a way to get her to smile today. A real smile, like the one she gave me yesterday in front of her family at the ugly sweater party. It felt like something was changing between us, like the possibility of 'us' could be real.

Maybe that was just wishful thinking on my part, and Phoebe was playing nice in front of the entire block of family and friends.

My alarm finally goes off. It's officially time to get up, get ready, and head to the Andrews' house to find out the last task. If we win this one, Phoebe will finally be crowned, and I want that more than anything. Well, maybe not anything. I'd like to be able to call Phoebe mine for the rest of my life, but baby steps.

I grab my phone to turn off my alarm when I see three missed calls from Austin and two missed calls from Piper. My first thought instantly goes to the worst thing imaginable: someone is hurt or possibly dead. With shaking fingers, I call Austin back. While I wait for him to answer, I mentally start praying that Mom and Dad are okay, that Phoebe is okay, and that her parents are okay.

Please, let everyone be okay, and let this be another one of those 'I'm overexaggerating' moments.

The call goes to voicemail, and I curse. Instead, I call Piper back to see if she answers. Does anyone not text anymore? Not one person left me a text. If something major has happened, I'd expect a text. I take a few deep, steadying breaths while waiting for Piper to answer. When she finally does, I feel like I'm about to pass out from relief while feeling a new wave of panic in my gut because I don't want to know if it's terrible.

"Hey, Stone-man!" Piper yells loudly. "What's up?"

"What—what do you mean 'what's up'? I have a million missed calls from you and Austin. You tell *me* 'what's up'!" My heart beats out of my chest, and I feel lightheaded and worried. "Is everyone okay? Please just tell me everyone is okay. Please," I beg her.

Piper chuckles loudly over the phone, making my ears ring. She must be in the car.

"Of course, everyone is okay. Your mind goes real dark after a few missed calls," Piper laughs. "We were just calling to tell you to meet us at the high school gym. Dad has the next task ready, and he told us to make sure everyone knows to meet him there. So I'll see you there!" She chirps, then promptly hangs up on me.

I look at the time and jump out of bed. The high school is about fifteen minutes away from our family's houses, and I'm going to be late if I don't hurry.

Less than 45 minutes later, I'm throwing open the door to the gymnasium. I'm *barely* late, just barely—only six-ish minutes or so. But Phil's smug smirk tells me Mr. Andrews has been keeping time. Phoebe has her back turned away from me, and I see she's talking animatedly to Piper, who has a giant smile.

I'm guessing Piper hasn't talked to her yet because I couldn't imagine them being so content and chummy together if she had.

Sisters or not, I'm very worried about the fallout that's bound to happen once Piper tells Phoebe the truth about everything.

Because it's either going to blow over like no big deal, or it's going to end up blowing their relationship to smithereens.

My chest feels tight at the thought of that happening, and as I walk closer to the group huddled in the center of the court, I realize that maybe it's best if Piper doesn't tell her.

Maybe it's time I let these feelings go, even if thinking about that makes my heart feel like it's being put through a paper shredder.

"You're late, Larson," Mr. Andrews says gruffly.

"He's like barely late, Dad," Phoebe chimes in, surprising me when she throws a wink my way. "It's the last task, and you changed the location on us at the last minute. Spencer lives the furthest away. Give him a break. Please?"

Phoebe wraps her arm through Mr. Andrews' and smiles sweetly at him. I have to hold back a smile when I see him roll his eyes in defeat.

He sends an unamused look my way.

"Alright, but because you were late, you and Phoebe get one hour taken away. It's the only way I can make it fair for the rest of the competitors who bothered to show up on time," he tells me. "You both have to have your task finished and ready by 5:00 PM tonight. The rest of you have until 6:00 PM."

Phoebe thanks her dad and then stands next to me on the outer circle of the center court.

"Thanks for that," I whisper to her.

"Don't mention it. Just be ready to run because we have to win this one." She smiles smugly at me, and we return our attention to Mr. Andrews.

He shoves his hands into his pockets and sways back and forth on his feet, making eye contact with every one of us before finally opening his mouth to speak again.

"Alright, kids, this is the final task of this year's Mistletoe Feud and the biggest challenge we've ever coordinated. Today is the town's Christmas parade, and your task will be to put together a float to drive through this year's parade. Spencer and Phoebe, you will use Spencer's truck. Phil and Kevin, I'm allowing you to borrow my truck for this one. Austin and Piper have been granted use of Mr. Larson's truck," he instructs us.

"You may rent a flatbed trailer or use the truck as your float base. Just please do not damage any of the vehicles. Especially my truck," Mr. Larson says with a glare directed toward Phil and Kevin.

Piper raises her hand.

"What do we use to decorate these floats? I don't think any of us have a float's worth of craft supplies hiding in our closets. Am I right?" She laughs nervously as she looks at all of us.

Mrs. Andrews answers her. "The community center is putting on this year's parade and graciously provided all the supplies for each participant. You have to head there and check out what you need."

Perfect. Now, we just need to plan a float, decorate it, and have it ready to roll by 5:00 PM. There is nothing stressful about this whatsoever.

Suddenly, Phoebe's hand is grabbing mine, and she's pulling me out of the gym as quickly as her slender body can take us. "We don't have much time, and I want to beat them to the community center so that Piper and Phillip don't take all the good stuff!"

Her laughter is contagious, and her hand fits perfectly in mine as we rush to my truck.

It's going to be so hard to let her go.

CHAPTER TWENTY-FIVE

Phoebe

Spencer and I are the first ones to make it to the community center, so we have first dibs on whatever supplies are available. We rush out of the truck and run inside like a bunch of teenagers sneaking around after curfew and trying our best not to get caught.

We've talked about a few potential float ideas on the short drive over, and we've narrowed it down to three options:

1. Whoville / The Grinch and Cindy-Lou-Who

2. Santa's Elves

3. The Nutcracker and Ballerina

Depending on what we can find, we can make any of these ideas work. With Spencer's handy skills and my decorative and art skills, we've got this in the bag.

The weirdest part of all this is that I don't care if we win anymore. I mean, I do, obviously. I've never won the crown, and I'd love to win it, but it's no longer my top priority.

I'm having more fun putting these tasks together with Spencer than I've ever had with anyone. Sure, he's nice to look at, and he's got that whole Greek God thing going for him.

But getting to know this older, more sophisticated version of him has been such a treat.

Plus, I think I'm sort of in love with the guy—and I'm not sure when I should tell him.

I don't want to ruin the comradeship we have had going on since being partnered together. Well, aside from our weird fight. Now that I know why he refused to tell me the truth about his and Piper's kiss all those years ago, there's this huge weight lifted off of my shoulders.

The tortured feelings I've had for Spencer aren't torturous any longer.

They are endless, limitless—invading my every breath and living in my bones.

Being with Spencer is like finally coming up for air after gasping for breath for years. Every subtle brush of our bodies, an accidental touch of our fingers, and lingering gaze make me feel alive. For the first time in my life, I feel like I'm finally being seen by him.

He's been telling me over and over that it's always been me, but up until this morning, I couldn't believe him. Not until he rushed into the gymnasium, and his eyes found mine. The look he gave me made me feel complete and entirely his.

I look up at him as we browse all the craft supplies the community center has left over. It's much more than I expected them to have, especially since I know the parade participants have been working on their floats over the last few weeks. Spencer's eyebrows are knitted together in concentration as he rummages through dozens of plastic totes full of Christmas decorations. As I gaze at him, I notice a small cardboard structure hiding in the corner. It looks like a small house, a little bigger than a dog house would be, but it needs some massive TLC. It's one of those houses that kids can decorate and turn into their own little in-home shops. It's perfect.

I nudge Spencer and point at the tiny house.

"What if we scrap all our ideas and make a gingerbread house? We could slap some paint on it and use white felt sheets on the roof, making it look like snow," I gesture to the bins around us.

"And we can use some of these decorations, along with the ones at your house, to make it look like the cutest little gingerbread house ever," I say thoughtfully as I beam up at him. "What do you think?"

Lost in thought, he brings his hand to his chin as he peers around the rest of the area. When he looks at me, I can see the excitement building in his eyes, and I know he's on board. "Let's do it! I'll grab the house, you get the white felt, and let's grab some of this garland. We can drop this stuff at home, run to Walmart, and grab some spray paint and whatever else we might need." Spencer's voice is full of enthusiasm, and it makes me feel flush with happiness.

"We gotta hurry," he says hushedly, forcing me to lean in closer to him. "The enemy has arrived." He gestures towards the door, and I see Phil and Kevin walk in.

We all freeze in place, and then Phil and I sprint, grabbing as much as possible before the other snags it.

Spencer comes running out behind me with the small house in his hands. He yells a loud 'thank you' to the ladies at the front desk, and we throw everything into the back of the truck as quickly as possible.

I hold out my fist to Spencer, and as soon as we get back into the truck, he fist-bumps me. The smile he gives me could battle the brightest of Christmas lights.

"We've got to move faster, Spence!" I yell as we barrel down the main road to town, my legs bouncing uncontrollably in my seat. It's 4:50 PM, and we are about 5-ish minutes from the main square downtown, where all the floats are supposed to line up. Dad texted me an hour ago and said he would meet us there to make sure we get our float clocked in on time.

"If I go any faster, then I risk the top of our gingerbread house flying away," Spencer says with gritted teeth while pressing down lightly on the gas.

We've worked nonstop all day to get this float done. It's not perfect, but from afar, she's a beauty. We spray-painted the house a light brown to make it all match; then Spencer stapled the white felt to the roof and laid some in the truck bed, so it looks like the house is on top of the snow, with some snow on the roof, too. I used the garland to make windows and the battery-powered Christmas lights to line the roof with makeshift garland windows. A red pool noodle makes up the arched door, and we used a small paper plate that I painted to look like a peppermint candy as the doorknob. We threw on more random holiday decor, and I painted more plates to look like various types of candy to decorate the rest of the house and the outside of Spencer's truck.

It's not perfect, but it's pretty great for only a few hours.

And the best part is that I found gingerbread man and woman onesie pajamas at Walmart, which Spencer and I will wear during the parade. Spencer has agreed to drive the truck while I toss little goodie candy bags to the crowd.

Our gingerbread house float may not win, but I'm so proud of us that I don't care. I've had so much fun with Spencer today. We've spent all day laughing and decorating, throwing paint and other stupid decor at each other while putting the float together.

There was no awkwardness or strained feelings, at least none on my end, now that I know what I want.

Just endless laughter and effortless fun.

The only tension that filled the room was the good kind of tension...if you know what I mean. All I want to do is scream to the rooftops about how much I want him, need him, crave him entirely. But I promised myself last night that I would wait until this competition was over before I shared my true feelings with Spencer.

And I'm hoping that night is tonight.

I fly back to New York after Christmas, which is only two days away. Depending on what Spencer feels, this could be my last trip to the Big Apple.

I don't want to get too excited about what could happen. Right now, I need to focus on the parade and then finally, hopefully, make Spencer mine. The rest will work out the way it's meant to.

Spencer taps my thigh, jarring me out of my fantasy.

"Hey, there's your dad. We just barely made it with no more than a minute to spare," he smiles brightly at me as he pulls into the parking lot with most of the other floats.

I jump out of the truck and hug Dad.

"What do you think?" I ask him, nervous as all get out because Dad dislikes sugarcoating things. "About the float, I mean. Do you like it?"

Dad crosses his arms and takes a lap around the truck, inspecting everything with keen eyes and a no-nonsense posture. He stops at my side, and I leap with joy when I see the slight smile sneaking over his lips. He likes it.

"It looks great, Pheebs. I can't believe you two pulled this off in just a few hours. You are some sort of dream team," he grins knowingly at me and throws his arm around me, giving Spencer a firm handshake. "Good job, kids. A gingerbread house is the perfect addition to the parade."

"Thanks, Dad. We had a great time putting this together, and I can't wait to see what the others are working on," I tell him.

He chuckles as he pulls his arm off of me. "You two got about an hour to kill before everyone gets lined up for the parade. Why don't you grab a bite or something to kill the time? I'll call you when it's time to come back."

Dad kisses my head and gives Spencer another handshake before he turns and heads back towards the other floats.

It isn't a far walk to the Christmas market, so I loop my arm through Spencer's, and we both head towards the main road together. I think this might be what I love most about being with him. I don't have to force myself to fill the silence because even in our silence, I don't feel alone.

CHAPTER TWENTY-SIX

Spencer

I swear I've put some sort of curse on myself.

I cursed myself the moment I decided to do the right thing and stop this nonsense of practically begging Piper to tell Phoebe the truth. Since then, Phoebe has made it nearly impossible for me to stick to my guns. We've been stealing subtle touches and heated glances back and forth all day.

It's like she woke up this morning and decided she didn't need the truth anymore, almost as if she's chosen to let the past stay in the past and be with me the way we should have been from the start.

But that doesn't happen in the real world, and even if today she decided to let it go, days, weeks, hell, months from now, she would inevitably bring it up again, and we'd go back to where we started.

It's torture.

Every moment in her presence today has been absolute torture.

And yet, I've loved every second of it, and I don't want it to end.

"What do you feel like doing until we go back?" Phoebe's voice floats up to me. "We could get something to eat, or maybe just grab something warm to drink and sit somewhere and talk?"

I look down at her, and the sight of her nearly brings me to my knees. How is it possible that we've spent all day building, creating, and decorating an entire float, and she still looks as perfect as she did when I walked into the school gym this morning?

Not a hair out of place or a paint stain to be seen. Her bright green eyes look like they're shining just for me, and the small smile on her lips should be every man's dream to see reflecting at them.

Phoebe squeezes her arm tighter around mine. "Earth to Spence, did you hear me?"

"Uh...I'm sorry. What did you ask?" I give her a sheepish smile because I blacked out every word she said when my eyes reached hers.

She chuckles softly. "I asked what you wanted to do while we waited. Dad said we have about an hour before we have to be back to line up."

"I filled up on too much candy while we decorated, so no food. Unless you're hungry?" Phoebe shakes her head at me. "What about a drink?"

She looks up at me and rolls her eyes. "You have to drive the truck through hundreds of adoring fans while I balance in the bed and toss out treats. Drinking and driving doesn't sound like a good time."

She's right.

"Want to go ice skating?" She asks nervously while her grip on my arm tightens. She refuses to look back at me, but I know she's gnawing at her bottom lip.

I gently grasp her chin, turning it towards me to see her face. She's definitely biting on her lip, and it's taking every ounce of self-control not to bend down and bite it for her.

Instead, I internally calm myself and grin back down at her. "I would love to go ice skating again with you, Phoebe."

Her nervous gnawing turns into one of her beautiful, breathtaking smiles. "Really? Even after our last attempt ended so horribly?"

I run my thumb across her cheek softly.

"You know how much I love second chances. I love to work hard until I've perfected my craft," I tell her.

And like the masochistic idiot that I am, I pull her face closer to mine and whisper in her ear, "Any type of craft. Whether ice-skating or using whatever I have at my disposal to bring pleasure to your life, I love to do it until it's perfect."

When I pull away from her, I notice her breathing is slightly heavier, and her pupils are wide as she gazes up at me. I smirk at her before grabbing her hand and intertwining her fingers with mine.

What I wouldn't do to whisk her away and bury myself in her.

She squeezes my hand, and we both head towards the ice rink. As we get closer, Phoebe slows down and then stops in her tracks completely. "What if we just go grab a room across the way?" She points at the small Bed and Breakfast across the street and flashes me a sultry smile that threatens to undo me.

Is she serious right now?

No. Absolutely not.

She can't be serious.

"Well?" Phoebe raises an eyebrow at me, making this feel like a dare.

And hell, if I'm going to turn down a dare, especially with her looking at me like she wants nothing more than to rip my clothes off and have her way with me.

"Lead the way, Phoebe," I smugly say. But my confidence falters as soon as the words are out of my mouth.

"Wait," I tell her. I take her other hand in mine and place my forehead against hers. "Don't get me wrong, this is literally a dream come true for me. But I don't want our first time to be like this. We've worked so hard on this float, and I'd be so angry at myself if I didn't get us to the end of this thing. Winners or not. I can't let you throw all this away for what I can guarantee will be a *quick lay.*"

She lets out a small chuckle.

"And I care about you too much. Too damn much, Phoebe. I don't want whatever this is between us to be just sex. That would devastate me."

And I also don't want to come between you and your sister.

Phoebe pulls her hands out of mine and places them against my cheeks, pulling me down and kissing me softly. "Piper already told me everything, Spence."

I pull back in shock and stare down at her. My mouth opens and closes like a gaping fish because I have so much I want to say, but my mouth can't seem to form the words.

"It's okay. None of that matters to me now. I understand why you both lied to me, even if I hate that I spent years thinking I was just some backup version of Piper, thinking that you wanted her," Phoebe says glumly, but with a small smile tugging on the corners of her mouth. "I want this. I want us. Whatever this is between us, it's not just some quick lay to me. It means so much more than that. You mean more to me than that."

She reaches up and caresses my cheek. "You're all I've ever wanted."

"I never—I never wanted her, Phoebe. It's always been you. It's *only* been you. I wanted to tell you the moment it happened, but I couldn't stomach the idea of you and Piper being angry with each other. It was easier for you to be angry at me because you still had her in your court. And she wasn't ready to tell you, so I vowed to keep her secret until she was. I'm so sorry I lied to you this whole time. Not being able to tell you the truth when you finally asked the other day was one of the hardest moments of my life. I knew keeping her secret meant losing everything between us, but I couldn't betray either of you like that," I confess.

It feels incredible to get this off of my chest now. All these years of wondering what my life could be like if I could tell Phoebe the truth. Well, it was miserable. And now that she knows? I could die and go to Heaven right now, except I'm too selfish, and I know a lifetime with her by my side wouldn't be enough.

"Thank you for keeping her secret. Knowing that you did that for her means the world to me. I wish you guys would have found another way to do it, but I understand. I'm just so happy that you weren't secretly pining after my sister this whole time we were hooking up." Phoebe laughs. "That was a real mind-screw for me, Spence. I never want to feel that way again, and honestly, I feel stupid for ever feeling that way in the first place. I guess I should have listened to one of the hundred times you told me you wanted me, huh?"

Her embarrassed smile might be the cutest thing I've ever seen.

"Do you believe me now when I say I've only ever had eyes for you?" I ask her with a cocky grin on my face that I can't seem to contain.

"I'll believe you if you kiss me and never stop." She takes a step closer to me and her hands grip the sides of my winter coat, pulling me down as she stands on her toes to reach me. "You only have about a half hour to do it before we return and win our Mistletoe crowns. So, let's hurry it up, handsome."

"Yes, ma'am," I whisper. Then I press my lips to hers softly, and she molds herself to my body completely.

This should have been our first kiss—the kiss that should have been ours all those years ago.

But life doesn't always work out the way you plan it. Sometimes, unknown obstacles throw themselves in the middle of those self-made plans, and all you can do is hope that it'll all work out in your favor.

And sometimes, a girl with gingerbread earrings tells fate to go screw itself and makes her own version of your plans work out even better than you could have ever hoped for.

CHAPTER TWENTY-SEVEN

Phoebe

Seeing Spencer dressed as a gingerbread man is seriously one of the best things in the world, and you best believe that I've already snapped a photo of him in his cute little onesie and set it as my phone background.

I can't stop smiling and laughing while I toss out our little goodie bags during the parade. Spencer talked his dad into driving the truck for us so we could both be in the back with our little house. I haven't let go of his hand since we got up here, and I can't stop looking over at him during our slow journey through the streets of Noelsville.

My entire body is ready for this parade and contest to be over with so I can drag him back to his house and really have my way with him. I wasn't exactly kidding when I told him I wanted to ditch this thing and spend the rest of the night tangled up in the Bed and Breakfast across the street. However, I'm also not upset that he talked some sense into me. My libido has been in overdrive since we finally confessed our true feelings to each other, and she's not calming down anytime soon.

"Did you see the other floats?" Spencer asks me over the loud Christmas music blasting over the town speakers. "Piper and Austin just decorated a tree and stuck it in the bed of their truck."

I watch as Spencer points to one of the red trucks a few car lengths behind us.

I scoff loudly.

"Piper doesn't really care to win this thing, does she? I can't even find Phil and Kevin. I wonder if they're somewhere ahead of us." I look ahead of us and don't see them.

Spencer squeezes my hand lightly, sending waves of fireworks throughout my body again. Every time he touches me, I want to explode into a billion little firecrackers of pure joy.

"I have it on good word that Kevin and Phillip have dropped out of this task," he says smugly.

I knit my eyebrows at him in question, and he laughs loudly.

"Kevin may or may not have accidentally backed your dad's truck up into the mailbox as they were leaving to pick up a trailer," Spencer shrugs as if it's no big deal, and I can't contain the gasp that escapes me.

"Please tell me he didn't do it on purpose. Dad is going to strangle him." As I say this, we see my parents, Spencer's mom, and Kevin hanging out on the side of the street, waving and cheering as the floats drive by. Dad doesn't seem upset, but Phillip looks like a sullen child who got coal for Christmas.

When Dad sees us, he smiles wide, holds up the coveted Mistletoe crown, and tosses it my way. Of course, I have the catching ability of a two-year-old, so it goes flying past me, and I watch as Spencer grabs it out of the air like a pro. I look back at Dad, and he's clapping along with the rest of the family.

Oh my gosh, *we won*.

We freaking won!

I feel a tap on my shoulder and see Spencer standing closer to me, twirling the crown around his finger. "What did you say earlier about not caring if we won?"

He's smiling *my* smile, and I throw my arms around him and kiss him soundly in front of the entire town. Not giving a single care who sees us.

When we break apart, Spencer places the crown on my head while wearing another one of those crooked smiles I love so much.

"Thank you for everything. For being the brilliant, talented, beautiful person that you are. This has been the greatest Christmas of my life, and I'm so glad I get to spend it with you," he whispers. His hands cup my face, and his thumbs wipe away the tears sliding down my cheeks. The look he's giving me makes me feel like we are the only two people on the planet right now. "I love you, Phoebe."

I'm pretty sure my heart just floated away, and this must be Heaven. How is this my life? A few weeks ago, I could have never imagined that this would be a part of my future, of our future. After years of feeling lost and adrift in New York, I finally found what I was looking for, and it was right here, waiting for me in Noelsville.

He was waiting for me.

I look up at Spencer. This amazing, incredible hunk of a man, and say the words that I've wanted to scream at him since I met him a billion years ago, "I love you, too."

We exchanged gifts after the celebratory dinner with our families and the official announcement that we had won the Mistletoe Feud this year. I'm proud to say that in addition to winning the Mistletoe crown this year, I also win at giving the best gifts ever.

While Spencer and I were shopping for supplies for our float, I saw the perfect gift for my parents. Or, I should say *purrfect* gift. My parents are now owners of two matching adult-sized gingerbread man Christmas sweaters, and Little E has his very own matching one. The three of them look adorable in their matching outfits as they wave to us as we pull out of the driveway.

On the drive back to my parent's house after the parade, Spencer and I decided I wasn't spending another night away from him.

I'll fly back to New York in a few days with an extra passenger added on. Spencer said he wanted to see New York, and I told him I wanted him to kiss the crap out of me in Times Square during the ball drop on New Year's Eve.

The rest we will figure out.

Tonight, though, is for us. There is a giant "Do Not Disturb" sign on the door.

We don't even make it through the door before we're all over each other. Spencer's eager hands grip the zipper of my ginger-bread onesie, and he tugs it down slowly. When his cool hands graze my chest, I shudder, grab the back of his head, and kiss him deeper as I tug his zipper down in return.

"Couch or bed?" Spencer asks with a shaky breath, his hands never leaving my body.

"Bed, then maybe the couch later. I plan on spending all night corrupting you and bringing you to the dark side," I say in the most sultry voice I can muster. It's difficult when my breathing is erratic, and my heart is pounding loud enough to drown out every coherent thought in my head.

"Bed it is," he says as he picks me up and wraps my legs around his waist, taking us both to his bedroom.

It doesn't take long before we've pulled every shred of clothing off each other, and it's just us, skin to skin, laying together under the duvet. I've already seen all of him, but this feels more intimate than any of our previous hookups. Maybe because now I know this is real and that it isn't all going to disappear in a puff of smoke as soon as this vacation is over.

"Hey, beautiful. What's going on in that head of yours?" Spencer asks quietly as he draws circles up and down my back while I'm sprawled across him.

I place several kisses on his arms, shoulders, neck, and jaw until I'm kissing him reverently on his lips.

"I'm just thinking that I talk a lot of smack for someone extremely nervous right now," I tell him, my voice shaking.

He gently tugs my chin up so I'm looking at him.

"We don't have to go further than where we are right now. I'll be happy to hold you all night long," Spencer promises.

"Oh no, I want this. I want you. I'm just feeling shy, I guess? It feels like this is epically more important than anything else we've done together," I say as a blush creeps over my face.

"Well, as the virgin in the bed, cuddled up with the most beautiful woman I've ever laid eyes on, who is totally naked, I might add. I am *extremely* nervous that I will let you down and you'll decide that my lack of skills isn't worth your time. Then you'll sneak out of bed and head back to New York without bothering to even leave a note on the counter."

I reach up and flick his nose, making him gasp and laugh.

"I would never do that to you. And I'm not expecting some wild night in the sack. I want you, however you'll have me." I run my hands down his torso, stopping just below his belly button.

"For however *long* you'll have me." I wiggle my eyebrows at him in jest, making him howl in laughter.

And just like that, the shyness and hesitancy vanishes. Spencer's laughter fuels the longing in me, and I reach lower, grabbing him in my hands and pumping him several times. He sucks in a shocked breath through his teeth and then pounces on me. Running his hands over my breasts, then circling each nipple with his fingers, then his tongue. My back arches and a moan of pleasure forces its way past my lips.

His hands start to trail lower and lower until he's also using them to pleasure me the way I am him. I use my free hand to pull him back up to me, kissing him forcefully and passionately. Our hands explore every part of our bodies while our lips refuse to break apart.

Spencer breaks away first and places his sweat-slicked forehead against mine.

"I'm not going to last much longer if you keep teasing me like that," he groans. His breath is coming in labored pants, and his heart is beating hard against my chest.

I use my hand to guide him to my entrance, never breaking eye contact with him. His pupils are wide, and our quick breaths are in sync.

"Are you on the pill, or should I grab a condom?"

"I'm on the pill, and I haven't been with anyone in a year. I'm okay with not using a condom if you are," I answer in return.

He flashes that crooked smile I love so much, and then his lips are back on mine as he pushes into me. We both moan against each other as I pull him as far into me as he can go, which is much, much further than I expected. I knew the man was blessed, but feeling it like this is intense and deep. He hasn't even started moving, and I already feel like I'm the one ready to explode.

Then he starts moving slowly and steadily in and out while I can feel every inch of him. It's erotic and sexy, and I never want this to stop. I grab onto him and grind myself against him in a silent plea to go faster. I'm close already, and the moment he puts his hand between us and presses his thumb to my core, I explode around him. Waves and waves of searing pleasure flood my body as I yell out his name. I claw into his back and bite down hard on his shoulder, and moments later, he finds his release.

We both lay intertwined, breathing heavily as the aftershocks of our orgasms rock through our bodies. Spencer lays his forehead on mine, and I struggle to open my eyes.

"I love you," he whispers against my skin, tattooing the words onto my soul. "Was that okay?" His voice is slightly nervous as he catches his breath against me.

"That was everything. Perfect. Amazing. All the great things." My voice is quiet but firm. "And baby, it'll only get better from here."

I smack his gorgeous ass loudly, making us both laugh.

Spencer kisses me again before he pulls out and settles himself next to me, throwing his arm around me and snuggling in close. "I can't imagine anything being better than that."

"Give me a couple of hours, and I'll show you some fun new positions that involve your couch and possibly some *Game of Thrones* episodes playing in the background." I wink at him, earning another burst of laughter from him. "Oh! Speaking of *Game of Thrones*, I have a really dumb gift for you."

I jump out of bed, pulling the sheet with me as I rush to the bathroom to clean up, and then I make my way to the living room in search of my purse. I grab the two wrapped-up ornaments and quickly walk back to the bedroom.

When I return to the bedroom, Spencer has two wrapped gifts sitting beside him.

"Since we are exchanging gifts, I figured I'd give you mine too," he says sheepishly.

"They're also really dumb, but I saw them, and they made me think of you." He hands them to me, and I give him the wrapped-up ornaments. "Open them together?"

I nod my head and grab the first gift. It's clearly some type of liquid because I can hear it sloshing around as I rip the green Christmas tree wrapping paper off it. I giggle when I see that it's a bottle of Fireball.

"Thank you, dear. It's just what I wanted. Another hangover in a bottle," I tease and bend over to give him a chaste kiss. "It's perfect, thank you."

Spencer smiles as he works on opening his first gift. Mr. Conrad knows how to wrap his ornaments up so they won't break in transit. When he finally opens it, he looks at the hot dog ornament in confusion.

"Open the second one, and it'll make sense, I promise."

He rips open the second gift, and when he sees the little Iron Throne, I start singing the theme song, well, my wiener version of it, and his entire face lights up before he bursts into the loudest fit of laughter I've heard from him.

"Phoebe, this is so stupid, and I love it so much. I'll cherish my Wiener Throne for the rest of our lives," Spencer boasts loudly. "Now hurry up and open yours. I think I'm ready to go try that couch position."

He shoots me a sultry smile and winks at me as he hands me a large, flat, square gift.

I tear the corners, and my hand flies to my mouth when I see the gift. "Spencer, did you really buy me a Taylor Swift vinyl *and* Fireball for Christmas? Are you trying to recreate our first night spent together?"

"They both just reminded me of the greatest night of my life," he says quietly, all laughter gone.

"The night you got your first blow job?"

He tosses the gifts to the side and pulls me into his lap, holding me close against him as he whispers into my ear, "No, well, yes, that too. But no. It reminded me of the night you finally decided I was worth a second chance."

I have no words because that might be the sweetest gift I've ever gotten from anyone. Instead of responding, I turn and kiss him with every single ounce of love and gratitude I have for him, which is endless.

I'm so glad I decided to come home for the holidays this year.

The Mistletoe Feud 2023 Standings:

Task One: The Christmas Market Salesman
WINNER: PHOEBE

Task Two: Surviving the Snow-Fort
WINNER: PHIL & KEVIN

Task Three: The Battle of the Gingerbread
WINNER: PIPER & AUSTIN

Task Four: Ugly Sweaters Make Life Better
WINNER: PHOEBE & SPENCER

Task Five: Floating Around the Christmas Parade
WINNER: PHOEBE & SPENCER

ACKNOWLEDGEMENTS

Who would have thought I'd be writing the acknowledgments for my second novel so soon after I released my first? Certainly not me, but I had a whole village of people who cheered me on and supported me every step of the way. This book wouldn't have happened without you.

Zach, thank you for putting up with my loud keyboard clicks in the middle of the night for what felt like endless evenings. Spencer Larson wouldn't exist without you, and I'm forever thankful to have such an amazing, wonderful man to model my fictional characters on. You light up my world in a way that nobody else can.

Annabell, one day, when you're old enough to read my books, I hope you smile whenever I reference your favorite fluffy companion. Even if she is a menace, who loves to knock my Christmas trees down and lay on my keyboard as I'm trying to write.

Cassian, my favorite little snuggle buddy. Thank you for the endless sticky fingers and even messier kisses during the long days.

I love our days together, even if you have an uncanny knack for stealing my mouse when I'm not looking.

To my family and friends: Dad, Mom, Mom, Aaron, Marisa, Adrian, Damian, Mathayus, Ayla, Adalene, Jerry, Kim, Sarah, Lorilea, Enrique, Emma, Little E, Nancy, Larry, Melinda, Paul, Peyton, Sam, Chris, Taylor and Mila...thank you all for supporting me through this journey of mine. I appreciate you all for taking the time to read my stories and keeping it to yourself if you hate them, lol.

To my beta/early readers, Esther, Haley, Amber, Mary, Katherine, and Kayla: Thank you for helping turn my trash into something readable. And for sending all the hilarious reaction voice notes, texts, videos, etc. You all truly kept me going and made the release of my second novel so freaking exciting. I can't tell you, guys, how many times you made me smile like an idiot at my phone from all your kind words. I'm so glad you all love Phoebe and Spencer as much as I do.

To the Bookstagram and BookTok worlds, neither of my books would have been possible without all the kind feedback and unwavering support from so many of you. Thank you to every single one of you who has followed along with me on this journey. To every person who has shared, liked, or commented on any of my posts, you guys kept me going and are the true MVPs.

Zelda Elizabeth, you may drive me insane with your zooming zoomies and tendency to knock everything off my desk at the worst times, but you're cute and cuddly when you want to be. I love your sassy, fluffy little butt, and I can promise every book I write will have some sort of cat in it just for you.

Esther & Haley, my favorite weasels. When I say I couldn't have written this book without you both, I truly mean that. Thank you for all the pick-me-ups when I was feeling down about my own writing and for the never-ending voice notes during the days that I felt uninspired. Your faith in me and my stories has never wavered, and I'm so incredibly lucky to have you both in my life during this era. #WeaselTrip2024

Last but not least, let me say thank you to YOU as the reader. I am honored that you chose my book to pick up and read out of all the billions of novels out there. I hope that some part of this story resonated with you, and I hope that everyone can find a small piece of themselves within these characters. I'd love to hear what you think about it, good or bad, though I hope it's mostly good things! If it isn't too much, please think about leaving a review wherever you write reviews! Reviews are incredibly important for indie authors like myself, and I would genuinely appreciate it!

Love always,
Danielle

Danielle Morris

has been an avid reader her whole life and always dreamed of one day writing her own novels. She loves reading and writing about complex and flawed, but highly relatable characters that make you laugh, cry, and feel all the things.
If she's not reading or writing she's likely spending quality time with her husband and two kids. She loves starting her day with a good cup of coffee, traveling, and being creative in other areas.

Connect with her online @daniellemorriswrites